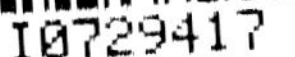

I0729417

Milk Chocolate KISSES

Cecelia Dowdy

Praise for
Cecelia Dowdy's Writing

Dowdy writes with the right touch to keep the readers engaged and vested…
- *USA Today*

CHAPTER 1

FRANKLIN REESE BANGED on the battered screen door. Where was everybody? As he pulled out his phone to check the time, he recalled the conversation he'd had with his boss that morning.

If the opening of the farm and ranch branch of their accounting firm proved successful…well…this could mean a partnership for him. Well, his boss didn't really *say* that but, he'd hinted. A partnership meant more money that he could use donate to a cause worthy of—

The loud bellow of a cow pierced the rancid air. He swallowed as he eyed the time. Nine o'clock. So, he wasn't late. He slid his phone back into his pocket. His stomach soured like curdled milk and his head pounded with pain. He needed to find the farmer and it appeared his new client may be in the barn with the bellowing cow. He might as well go find her. Taking a deep breath, he walked as fast as he could toward the barn. Another loud bellow pierced the air.

He approached the faded red barn and then stopped as soon as he spotted the big black and white cow suffering through a breach birth. Dumbfounded, he dropped his briefcase as he peered at the feet of the baby sticking out of the mother's bloody birth canal. A rope was looped around the legs of the young animal. A light brown woman pulled the rope so hard that the muscles in her slender arms flexed. Her eyes squeezed shut while she grunted, reminding him of the noises people made when they bench-pressed weights. She opened her eyes. "Casey, hold on," she cooed. As he watched the birth, his sour stomach worsened, and the bagel and cream cheese he'd managed to eat for breakfast felt like a dead weight in his belly.

Her tears mingled with the sweat rolling down her face. She continued to pull and glanced in his direction. "Oh, thank God you came. Come and help me."

Her light brown eyes pleaded with him. A plethora of unfamiliar scents tingled his nose. He swallowed, losing his voice. What was he supposed to do?

She continued to look at him, pulling on the rope periodically. "I already left a message on your answering service that it was coming out backward." Looked like he didn't have a choice. He may as well try to help her. This pretty farmer obviously had him confused with someone else, but, he couldn't focus on that right now. Pushing the door open, he entered the room adjoining the barn. His stomach clenched again. Hopefully, he wouldn't throw up. She nodded toward the rope, still tugging. "With both of us pulling, maybe we'll be able to get the calf out."

"Okay." He swallowed his nausea and pulled, mimicking the way he used to grunt when bench-pressing heavy weights. He followed her example, keeping tension on the rope and pulling each time the cow had a contraction. She grunted also, and their noises continued until the bloody calf slid out of the birth canal minutes later. She dropped the rope, and he rushed behind her to look at the young animal. He touched the newborn, awed by the birth. She glanced at him as she cleaned gunk off the calf's nose and mouth.

Her sigh filled the space when she noticed the animal was breathing. "Aren't you going to examine the cow and calf?"

Before he could respond, a young man holding a large black plastic tote entered the pen. "This the Cooper farm?"

She frowned and bit her lip as she glanced at him. She folded her arms in front of her chest as she quickly eyed Frank and the newcomer. The newcomer rushed to the baby cow and began examining it. "I'm Dr. Lindsey's son. I'm taking over my daddy's practice this week since he's on vacation. He told you that, didn't he?"

She nodded, still looking confused. "I left a message on your answering service earlier."

The vet grunted. "I was down the street at the horse farm helping out with another birth, so I couldn't leave."

"Are the cow and calf okay?"

"They both look fine." He stopped his examination and looked at them. "I'm glad you had somebody helping you. You might not have gotten him out in time if you'd been pulling him on your own." He pulled a tool out of his bag. "You have antibiotic on hand for the calf, right? If not, I've got some."

The attractive woman nodded, her dark hair clinging to her sweaty neck as she promised the vet she would give the new calf the medicine. Frank watched, mesmerized by the whole process. A short time later, the newborn nursed from the mother. "Thank you, doctor," said the woman, patting the man on the shoulder.

The doctor shook his head, placing his tools back into his bag. "Don't thank me. You two got him out in time." He hoisted his back. "Well, I've got another appointment. I'll send you your bill." Seconds later, the vet revved the engine of his battered pickup truck before speeding away.

She eyed Frank slowly, starting from his casual tan shoes, then to his khaki slacks and oxford shirt. She looked as if she'd never seen such clothing before. What was wrong with her? He supposed she'd been so busy birthing the cow that she'd not noticed that he wasn't dressed like a vet.

Noticing his bloody hands, she beckoned him

over to a room containing a sink and a large steel tank. After ripping off the long plastic gloves covering her hands and forearms and dropping them into the trash can, she turned the water on, pumped out several squirts of soap, and washed. "I thought you were the vet," she said, continuing to scrub her hands and forearms. "I've never met Dr. Lindsey's son, so that's why I assumed you were him." After rinsing, she pulled paper towels from a dispenser and gestured for Frank to use the sink.

Frank shrugged and walked to the sink, placing his hands under the running water. "Sorry. I helped you out, but I didn't have any idea if I was doing it right. It's probably good I showed up when I did. It looked like you'd been trying to help that cow for a long time."

She shook her head. "Cows are tough. They can be in labor for hours before giving birth. When you came, I'd just started pulling the calf out with the rope." She continued to stare, frowning. "Well, if you're not Dr. Lindsey's son, then who are you?" Good grief, it was downright ridiculous that she didn't seem to remember that she'd booked an appointment with his accounting firm. Maybe birthing that cow was making her forget about her financial affairs.

He offered his recently washed hand. He mentally sighed with relief. Good thing the nauseous feeling had evaporated from his stomach. He certainly didn't want to vomit on his attractive new client. "I'm Franklin Reese, Certified Public Accountant."

Emily ignored his hand, narrowing her eyes.

His adam's apple bobbed as he gulped. "Most folks call me Frank."

"You're from an accounting firm? You're kidding."

"Why would I kid about this?" He beckoned her over to his abandoned briefcase and slid the golden locks open, removing a sheaf of papers. He held the documents toward her. "It's all right here. You contacted us to come out here because you said you lost your bookkeeper and you needed somebody to show you how to properly do the accounting for your farm."

She shook her head, refusing to take the papers. Gritting her teeth, she recalled the countless arguments she'd had with her stepmother, Laura, during the last several weeks. "So, you're the accountant from Bryers and Ridge Accounting Firm that just opened in Dairy?" Laura had hinted that she'd been thinking about contacting the firm, but, Emily didn't think she'd have the guts to do it.

Looked like she'd been wrong. This time, she'd underestimated her stepmom and now she needed to do what she could to resolve this.

Laura just didn't understand that Emily needed more time to figure things out…more time and a lot of prayer. Heck, she'd been praying for a miracle the past few weeks…no way would God answer her prayer by sending this accountant to her door, would He?

Frank nodded. "The main office is at the Inner Harbor. They just opened this new branch to service the Dairy Maryland farm community."

She folded her arms in front of her. "I didn't call you. My stepmother did." No need to admit that she was totally against hiring him.

"Look. . .what's your name?" His mouth hardened into a thin line. Goodness, she was actually staring at him. His full, perfect lips and strong jaw, and deep, cocoa-brown skin. Heaven help her, he reminded her of the model she'd recently seen in a magazine. He raised his thick eyebrows as looked directly at her.

She forced herself to look away. She kicked a stone with the toe of her shoe before sliding her hands into the back pockets of her jeans. Maybe after the introductions she could sort this whole thing out.

"I'm Emily Cooper."

He still clutched the papers, frowning. "Did you want to call the office and reschedule?" He gestured toward the barn. "I see you've had a rough morning, so you might not be in the mood to talk about your finances right now."

"Just give me a second, okay?" She stepped away, noting how the cool scent

of his cologne wafted around her, teasing her nose. She removed her cell phone from her pocket and hit the speed dial to call Laura. Emily left her stepmother a message, clutching the phone and speaking in a low voice so that he wouldn't hear her. "Mom, I thought we'd agreed you wouldn't hire that accountant until we talked about it some more. He's here now, and I'm not sure what to do." She ended her message and placed her phone back into her pocket. She gazed at the silos in the distance, still wondering how to handle this situation. The heated arguments she'd had with Laura about hiring an accountant played in her mind like a broken record.

"Did you want me to leave and come back another time?"

She jumped when his deep voice sounded behind her. "What's the phone number for your firm?"

He held the papers toward her. She took the cream-colored stationery, noting the number on the top. She called and spoke with the secretary, who confirmed Frank's appointment.

She shoved her phone back into her pocket just as he presented her with a laminated ID card. "I usually show this as soon as I get to a new house. But since you were busy in the barn, my routine was messed up. Did you want to call the office back and reschedule?"

Shaking her head, she figured it was wrong of her to go against Laura's wishes. "No, come on." She gestured toward the house, wiping sweat from her brow. They walked to her home, and she opened the door and entered the shaded, screened-in porch. Emily removed her barn boots and noticed dung stuck on his footwear.

"Oh no." She cringed. "I'm so sorry." He glanced down at his feet and his eyes widened. She took a deep breath. What an awful morning. Frank was just doing his job – he had nothing to do with her quarreling with her stepmom. Plus, he'd helped her to birth the calf – and he wasn't even a farmer. She'd been so angry about his showing up against her wishes that she'd not taken time to properly thank him.

Her mother was probably scolding her from heaven. She touched his shoulder. "I feel bad about the mess on your shoes."

He shrugged, looked directly at her. Her heart skipped when he looked at her with his piercing dark brown eyes. "I'm not worried about my shoes. I just need to get started."

She mentally sighed. Whew. This man had a job to do. She figured he charged by the hour. Without her having to tell him, he removed his shoes. "I'm sure there's a hose or something around here to clean my shoes?"

"Of course." She took his shoes and rinsed them off. Good thing he was wearing sneakers. After leaving her boots on the porch, she told him to remove his shoes. They entered the kitchen, and she showed him the bathroom in the hallway. "You can wash up in there. I think I have some of my dad's clothes that you can wear so I can wash your shirt and shoes. You look like you're about his size." He shook his head. "No need. I was going to play basketball after work. I can change into my basketball clothes." He rushed to his car and returned with a gym bag. He quickly went into the bathroom and slammed the door. As soon as she heard the water running from behind the closed bathroom door, and she left to start a load of laundry.

When she returned to the kitchen a few minutes later, he exited the bathroom wearing a tank top, basketball shorts and high-topped sneakers. She tore her eyes away from his muscled arms and strong-looking calves. She figured he must shoot hoops daily to stay in such great shape. She swallowed, her throat suddenly dry. She simply felt uneasy because this man was in her home unexpectedly – he was invading her territory and she just wasn't used to someone coming in and taking charge like this. She pushed her feelings aside. She couldn't let this man know how unsettled she felt. "Your clothes are in the washing machine. When you leave today, I'll have everything done."

He waved her comment away. "Can you just show me where you keep your files?" My, he really seemed in a hurry to get started. Well, she may as well let him begin.

"They're in my father's office." She approached the closed door, hesitating before opening it. She took a deep breath, beckoning him to follow her into her dad's space. Her arms ached from pulling the calf earlier, and the effects of her sleepless night made her want to take a long nap. He glanced around before focusing on the filing cabinet. "Do you know where your father keeps his P&L statements?"

Emily frowned, looking around the cluttered room. "His what?"

"You know, his profit and loss statements. I've noticed that most small business owners use Quickbooks."

Emily shook her head. "We don't use Quickbooks." She turned on the laptop and quickly typed in the password. In minutes she'd access the files and showed Frank where the bank statements were stored.

The files were meaningless to her. The way her dad had accounted for everything…he didn't use software. Instead, he had a plethora of Excel files with formulas and macros and….she'd been so confused, trying to figure everything out for herself. She'd tried to teach herself accounting, had gone online and read a few articles, but, none of it made sense to her. She'd even purchased an accounting book from Amazon and had tried to read through it. Once, she'd stayed up half the night, trying to understand it, and Laura had come and urged her to go to bed.

He nodded. "Okay…thanks. How about his tax returns? That'll be a good place for me to start."

She winced. His tax returns. She'd been so busy struggling to understand her dad's bookkeeping methods that she'd not even thought about accessing his tax returns. This was way more than she could handle, but, if she just had more time, and prayed some more about it, she was sure that she could work this whole thing out without Frank's help. She took a deep breath, still wondering what to do.

He gestured toward the cabinet. "A lot of our clients keep paper copies of their returns. I'm assuming he filed his taxes online. Did he print out copies and put them in the filing cabinet?"

Emily glanced around the room. "I'm not sure."

"You don't even know where your tax returns are?" His voice cracked through the room like a whip. Sounded like somebody had woken up on the wrong side of the bed this morning. She mentally groaned, cringing as the exasperation in his voice settled around the room like dust.

She gritted her teeth. No way was she going to let him talk to her like that. She looked directly at him and narrowed her eyes. "No, I don't know." Wringing her hands, she assessed the piles of paper scattered around the office.

"Why did your stepmother call us for our

services if you don't know where the paperwork is?" He threw his hands up in the air. "I feel like I'm wasting my time here. You know we charge by the hour."

She snapped, again whipping her head toward him. "I'm sorry." She squeezed her hands together. "I don't know where anything is. You're welcome to look and charge us for your extra time." Hot tears pricked her eyes, and she turned away, not wanting him to see her cry. "I have chores to do in the barn." She turned and exited the house, welcoming the intense heat as she ran down the hill toward the barn.

Whew, now that was just terrible. He'd barked at the woman like an angry bull. No way was he going to get the partnership if he didn't work on his people skills. A wave of pain shot through his head like a bullet. He dropped into a chair, rubbing his aching head.

He popped his briefcase open and removed a bottle of water and some Tylenol from his briefcase and took the pills. He guzzled the entire bottle of water. Hopefully Emily's father would be around soon to help him find the files he needed. He closed his eyes and sighed. He needed to stop drinking so much every night.

A hangover. That's what he had. Alcohol helped

him to forget all that had happened to him over the past few years. He winced. Pain and loss. Booz was had helped to forget all of that, but, he had to deal with the consequences the next morning. He really needed to kick this habit. He didn't want his bad temperament to ruin his chances of getting the partnership. He sighed and opened his eyes and stood up and stretched. Wanting to take his mind off of everything for a while, he focused on the walls. Vivid framed posters of the beach covered the walls. He studied a sting ray diving through crystal clear blue water. Another pic was of a huge turtle swimming through a vivid aqua ocean. Then another picture displayed a colorful school of fish swimming through the sea. The photos were a blue oasis of color – just looking at them made him feel nice. The pics reminded him of the Tahitian vacation he'd taken with his folks when he'd been in high school. The beach had been magnificent and he'd had a wonderful time swimming with wildlife in the Pacific Ocean.

Well, enough daydreaming. Time to get to work. He plopped back into the chair and started going through the spreadsheets that Emily had accessed earlier. Perhaps he'd be able to find the tax returns on his own. He put on his reading glasses as he began to sort through the numbers.

As he scrolled through the spreadsheet, he wondered if his sudden move to Baltimore County had been a mistake. Well, they'd needed somebody for this assignment and with his pathetic excuse of a life, he figured the change would do him good. Maryland was a far cry from Chicago, and with the hint of a partnership… well, that was enough of an incentive for his move to another state. One of the perks that this employer offered was home visits to farms to do accounting. It was a service that many of the other firms did not offer, and their marketing department was hoping that this new branch would expand their firm into great new territory.

He mentally ignored the cows mooing from the fields and the smell of manure and hay as he worked through the spreadsheets. As he crunched numbers, it was like he was in a world of his own. As he added up the figures in the column of a spreadsheet, his stomach growled. He ignored the sound of a door slamming. Footsteps echoed from the kitchen. Maybe Emily, or her stepmom, had returned to the house.

He plugged his earphones into his ears and turned on some jazz music as he continued to crunch numbers. He'd stop for lunch once he was finished with this row of calculations. As he continued working, the scent of roasted nuts and chocolate wafted from the kitchen. His mouth watered.

Hot fingers clapped his shoulder. He jerked his head around and spotted Emily. Her hair was pulled back into a ponytail and a cowboy hat perched on her head. Her red eyes…droopy mouth…looked like she'd been crying. He ignored his spreadsheet and focused on her.

She took a deep breath. "I'm sorry I lost my temper with you earlier." She shrugged, and his heart skipped. The urge to do something, anything, to make her feel better erupted within him like a volcano.

Well, least he could do was let her know that it was his fault, too. "I'm sorry, too. I have a quick temper, and when people call us for services and don't have the proper paperwork, I get a little upset." The urge to rub her shoulder and let her know everything would be okay rushed through him. "Our admin is supposed to send a letter or an e-mail beforehand, confirming our appointment and letting you know what files you need to have ready."

She shrugged. "Either Laura got the e-mail and forgot to tell me, or your admin didn't send it."

"So, you're not sure where your father keeps his tax forms?" He glanced around the office. "Is he around to show me where they're filed?"

She shook her head, and her eyes filled with tears. She looked away for a few seconds and then turned toward him, wiping her eyes. "My father passed away a couple of weeks ago."

His heart skipped a beat. "I'm sorry." Shame, hot and thick as pea soup, rushed through him. He took a deep breath. Goodness knows it would've been better if he'd known this in advance. He wondered if her stepmom had failed to give their admin this information, or, if the admin had simply forgotten to let him know about this. "I didn't know."

"It's okay. I haven't been myself since he died. My stepmother's taken his death pretty hard, so she left a couple of days ago, and she's staying with her daughter in Florida until she feels better."

He frowned. "You don't know how long she'll be gone?"

She shook her head. "She already had this trip planned before Dad died. My dad and Laura usually go to visit her daughter every year at the same time. She should be gone at least a few weeks. I already left her a voice mail asking her to call me." She shrugged. "Laura's not one to check her phone or texts much. I left a message on her daughter's phone, too."

"Why are you against getting financial advice for your farm?" Why wasn't she saying anything? Well, he needed to make sure she understood how important this was. Since her dad died, he probably had not shared the importance of keeping accurate financial information. He popped his briefcase open and again looked at the documents.

"In addition to basic bookkeeping advice, your stepmom also wanted to have your farm audited."

"Audited? Why? I thought that was something the IRS randomly did to check up on taxpayers' returns."

He frowned. Looked like he had some

explaining to do. He placed the paperwork on the desk. "That's true, but people can hire accountants to audit their business to make sure they're following GAAP."

"GAAP?"

"Generally accepted accounting principles. For a farm or ranch, people might also want to know the net worth of their business. Your stepmother might want to know these things since your father is gone and she's not used to doing the bookkeeping." He gestured toward the computer. "Do you mind taking a look to see if you can figure out where your father stored his tax returns?"

"I can try."

"Do you know if he filed them online or if he hired somebody to help him?"

She shook her head as she made herself comfortable in a chair. "Dad did everything himself. He had a knack for numbers. I admired that about him."

He eyed her tapping on the keyboard, noticing her extremely short, unpolished nails. After searching for a few minutes, she opened the drawer and rifled through the contents, mumbling to herself. She pulled out a flash drive. "I mentioned to me once that he keeps his old tax returns here."

She snapped the flash drive into the computer. "I found his taxes, but, they're old." He scanned the documents. The tax returns were from six years ago. Well, it was better than nothing. He figured they'd find the rest of the documents he'd need soon enough.

She continued sitting beside him. Wisps of her dark hair escaped from her ponytail and rested on her slender neck. Realizing that he was staring, he forced his thoughts back to the job they were doing. "I'll look through the files on the flash drive. I don't want to keep you if you have things to do."

She nodded, the worried look evaporated from her face – looked like she didn't want to sit in the office with him. He could understand that since she probably had chores to do on the farm. "I have stuff to do in the barn."

"You're running this farm alone?"

She folded her arms in front of her. "Sort of. We do have two twin teenaged brothers who help us out. They live on the horse farm up the road, but they're not very responsible." He thought about payroll expenses, employment forms and other such documents. He wondered if Emily paid the teens under the table, or, if she properly recorded their salaries. He'd ask her about that later.

"They don't always show up for work?"

"No, they don't, and it's wearing me down." She gestured toward the laptop. "Laura and I never knew much about the finances of the farm, so when Dad died, we knew we needed a little bit of help for the chores, but we didn't want to go overboard and hire more help than we could afford. Darren and Jeremy, our teenage hired help, agreed to take turns helping me each day with the milking. Since it's summer, they have free time, and they each have other part-time jobs. One of them works at the Leonardo's."

"Leonardo's?"

"It's the only pizza place in Dairy."

Frank eyed her, trying hard not to stare. "Was one of them supposed to be here this morning?"

She narrowed her eyes. "Yes. When one of them doesn't show up and I confront them about it, Darren will always say he thought Jeremy was coming and Jeremy will always say he thought Darren was supposed to come." She shrugged. "One or the other comes often enough for it not to be a huge problem. That is, not until today. It really would have helped me a lot if one of them had shown up and helped me with the difficult birth." He silently agreed with her.

"Why didn't you want your stepmother to hire outside accounting help?" She'd dodged his question the first time. He needed to understand her hesitation so that he could better assist her. Maybe she'd had a bad experience with an accountant and was leery about working with them.

"I have my reasons." He assumed that was her way of saying it was none of his business. "But since you're here and my stepmother wants you here, then I guess you need to do your job."

As she turned to leave, he stopped her with a

comment. "Oh, I forgot to tell you earlier, Laura paid a deposit for our services. The office will send a final bill once the audit is completed."

She nodded. Once she left, he continued scrolling through her father's old tax returns. He then returned to the Excel documents he'd been studying earlier that day. A few hours later, he frowned. The numbers did not look accurate. He sighed. Emily had said her dad was a number cruncher, but, he obviously was no accountant. It was going to take some time for him to figure out the late Mr. Cooper's bookkeeping methods.

CHAPTER 2

A FLY WHIZZED IN front of her face and landed on her cheek. Emily swatted the fly away. The insect was just another annoyance in her long, hot, exhausting day. Her lips dried with thirst as sweat rolled down her back. She leaned back toward the hot sun, closed her eyes and stretched. She looked forward to a long cool shower and a good dinner later. Maybe she'd treat herself to dinner Leonardo's. The hole-in-wall restaurant served the best pizza. She knew for a fact that they had their tomatoes fresh-delivered each day, and she could taste the goodness in their sauce.

She checked her phone. Five o'clock. She rolled her tired shoulders and opened the gate of the huge barn, which doubled as their milking parlor, and let the cows into their stalls. The thirty large black-and-white animals stomped into the enclosure, each going into her space. "Hey, Emily."

She grinned with relief when Jeremy Dawson approached.

"I'm glad you finally showed up. I just finished cleaning the equipment for the milking and gave the cows their feed." She'd already attached the mobile milking units to the pipes so they could start milking the cows.

The lanky, mocha-colored teen ran his fingers over his newly cornrowed hair. "Didn't Darren come this morning?"

She folded her arms in front of her chest, frowning. "No. Your brother didn't show up."

"But I thought he was going to come."

"You boys really need to make up your schedule. I really needed you here today."

He followed her into the stalls. "Why, did something happen?"

"Yes, Casey had her calf, and it came out backward."

The young man winced. She put her gloves on and took out the white bucket of cleaning solution. He went into the back room to wash his hands then returned. "Did somebody help you?"

"I'll tell you about that in a second." He put on his gloves, and she handed him an iodine-filled dipper. After pressing the dipper against the udders of the first four cows, they wiped the iodine off the udders with a clean cloth. Then they turned the vacuum on and attached the mobile milking units to the four cows. As the machines milked the bovines, Emily and Jeremy worked together, cleaning the teats and udders of the next group of bovines.

One of the cows in the next group was especially dirty, so Emily cleaned the udders with the iodine and water solution in the bucket before using the dipper. She then focused on Jeremy. "Yes, somebody helped me. It took a long time." She then explained how she'd had to use a rope to get the calf out, and she mentioned that their new accountant arrived in time to help her.

They worked together, milking four cows at a time, moving the mobile units from cow to cow before reattaching the units to the milk pipes. The rhythmic thumping of the machines and the gentle *swish* of the white liquid going through the clear pipes soothed her frazzled nerves.

"So, you hired an accountant?" Jeremy unhooked one of the machines. Cats scurried around the barn as he moved the unit to the next cow. He turned the suction on and hooked the machine to the udders of the animal. She sprayed the recently milked cows' udders with disinfectant. She'd been praying all day about the strange, unsettled feeling she had about their new accountant. It just didn't seem right having an outside person doing their finances.

Couldn't she and Laura try to figure out the bookkeeping on their own? "Yes." She told him the name of the firm they were using.

He nodded. "Yeah, my mom and dad hired an accountant a couple of months ago."

"Really? Why?"

The teen shook his head. "I don't know. Something about the IRS and an audit or something." He shrugged. She made a mental note to ask Jeremy's mother about her experiences using an outside accountant the next time she saw her in church.

Jeremy continued to speak as he attached the machine to another cow. "You know, I heard my mama talking to somebody on the phone, and she said that you need to get married to get somebody to help you take care of your farm since your stepmom doesn't like farming and your daddy's gone."

Her mouth dropped open, staring at the young man. "Jeremy, you shouldn't be repeating your mother's conversations."

He shrugged. "She didn't tell me not to repeat what she said."

Blowing air through her lips, she prayerfully tried to suppress her anger at Jeremy's mom for spreading untrue gossip. She'd always assumed Laura didn't like farming as much as she and her dad did, but she'd never heard her say she didn't like farming at all. She wondered if Laura had confided to Jeremy's mother that she didn't like her husband's profession. She knew Laura would sometimes visit Jeremy's mother and they'd have coffee. Sometimes they volunteered for the same ministries at church.

She further wondered why Jeremy's mother

would even be talking about her single status. Since her breakup with her fiancé a year ago, marriage was the last thing on her mind. At twenty-eight, she felt her life was fulfilled just running the farm and trying to glean a profit from her family's business.

Once the milking equipment was cleaned and the cows, beef cattle, and bull were fed, she looked directly at Jeremy. "You can go home now. But make sure either you or your brother are here at five o'clock tomorrow morning for the milking."

He grinned, giving her a mock salute. "Yes, ma'am." He rushed down the hill toward his pickup truck.

Her stomach rumbled, and she returned to the house after finishing up the chores. The sound of Frank typing on her dad's computer behind the closed office door spilled into the hallway. She leaned against the wall and took a deep breath. Man, she needed to take a shower. It would be weird to take one with this strange man in her house. Her stomach growled again. Her mouth watered when she again thought about dining at Leonardo's. After quickly washing up at the sink, she removed Frank's clothing from the dryer. She needed to return his clothes to him before heading out to get something to eat.

When she approached the office, she caught Frank gathering his things to leave. He placed his glasses into the holder before slamming his briefcase closed. "I'll probably be back sometime tomorrow if that's okay with you."

"That's fine." She held his clothes up. "Here are your clothes. I forgot to give them to you earlier." She offered him the small pile of laundry.

"Thanks." He accepted his clothes and stuffed them into his briefcase.

She removed the keys from her purse and followed him onto the screened-in porch and locked the door. She got into her old, battered white pickup truck, and Frank unlocked the door to his burgundy Lexus. When Emily turned the key in the ignition, the engine sputtered, refusing to start. She repeated the gesture, pressing on the gas. The grinding turn of the engine filled the air before it sputtered and died. Laying her head on the steering wheel, she groaned. "Lord, please let this truck start."

Sweat rolled down her neck when she sat up, turning the key again. When the engine failed, Frank stuck his head into the open window of her truck. Relief flowed through her like warm honey. Thank God he hadn't left. She'd been so focused on starting her car that she'd not noticed that he hadn't yet driven away. Funny sensations danced in her stomach when he leaned closer staring at her dashboard. "Did you run out of gas?"

"No. I have plenty of gas." She sighed. "I can't get my truck to start."

He glanced at the pickup. "How old is this thing?"

"My dad bought it about fifteen years ago." She gestured toward the hood. "Whenever we had a problem with it, I'd always pop the hood, and he could fix it."

"I'm not very good with fixing cars, but I'll take a look." She pushed the button to pop the hood. She got out of the truck and joined him, looking down at the engine. The wires and inner workings were foreign to her, and the longing for her dad whisked through her, making her wish he were still alive. She blinked the sudden tears away, again focusing on the engine.

Frank tinkered for a bit before closing the hood. "I think you'll need to get a tow truck."

"I was afraid of that." Blowing air through her lips, she returned to the cab of the truck to retrieve her purse.

"Did you want to call a tow truck?"

"The auto shop down in Dairy is closed." She looked at her watch. "I'm going to call them for a tow tomorrow. They usually close around seven o'clock."

"Don't you have AAA? They'll send a tow out immediately."

She shook her head. "I've never needed AAA since I had Dad and the auto repair shop in Dairy."

"Can I give you a lift?"

She clutched the strap of her purse. "I don't

want to hold you up. I might be able to get Kelly or Christine to pick me up."

"Who are Kelly and Christine?"

"My best friends. But I think they're working late tonight."

He continued to look at her, pulling his car keys out of his pocket. "I don't mind dropping you off. Where were you going?"

"I was going to Leonardo's for dinner."

"Who's Leonardo? Your boyfriend?"

She giggled. "No, Leonardo's is a restaurant." She checked her watch, and her stomach grumbled. "I'm starved, and since Mom's been gone, I haven't done much cooking. I've been eating out a lot." She shrugged. "I'm a lousy cook."

He gestured toward his car. "I don't mind dropping you off."

"Well, if you're sure." She followed him to his luxury car and got in. He started the motor and turned on the air conditioning. He pulled out of the gravel driveway, and cool air filled the car. That air conditioning sure felt nice. "Ah, air conditioning."

He chuckled as he turned a corner and increased the temperature of the air conditioner. "You act like air conditioning is a luxury."

"Sometimes I feel like it is. The air conditioning in our truck conked out a few years ago, and we never got it fixed."

"Don't you have your own car?"

"I've never been able to afford a new car. I had

a used one for years, but it stopped working a month ago, and with Dad's death and everything, I haven't had time to try and replace it."

They soon pulled into the parking lot of the small strip mall where Leonardo's was located. She exited the car, surprised when Frank cut the ignition and got out of the vehicle. "I hope you don't mind my eating with you. I wanted to talk to you about the finances on your farm. Besides, you'll need somebody to drop you off after you eat." He retrieved his briefcase from the backseat, and when she glanced at the floor, she spotted a huge bottle of scotch and an empty vodka bottle. She frowned. Did he drink booze while he drove his car? He dropped the briefcase back onto the seat. "Would you prefer that I not eat with you?"

She shook her head, putting the image of the empty vodka bottle from her mind. His drinking while driving was none of her business…well, maybe it was her business. Would he be driving on these back-country roads, drinking hard liquor? They often had cow crossings in the middle off the road. What if he ran over something? He touched her arm. "What's wrong?"

She hesitated, bit her lip. She gestured toward his backseat. She barely knew this man, but, needed to know he'd behave himself and not drink if he were taking her home. She'd call a cab or one of her friends to come get her if he did get out of hand. "I noticed the empty vodka bottle in your backseat." She shrugged. "Just looked like you were one to drink while sitting in the car." Why else would somebody have an empty booze bottle in the car.

He sighed. "You don't have anything to worry about. I promise."

Well, that answered her question. She was making a big deal out of nothing. All they needed to do was have dinner and talk about her farm's finances. He'd drop her off at home afterwards. She nodded. "Okay."

He retrieved his briefcase before they entered Leonardo's. Tomatoes, garlic, and cheese scented the air, and Emily's mouth watered as he pulled his chair out for her. There were only two tables located in the carryout restaurant. He cleared his throat. He looked a little uncomfortable. She figured he didn't like her questioning his drinking. "Did you want to split a pizza?"

"Sure."

He approached the counter and returned with two Cokes. "They said the pizza will be ready in about twenty minutes. I ordered pepperoni and extra cheese with mushrooms. Is that okay?"

She nodded. "That's fine."

A group of rowdy teenagers entered and sat at the table across from them. At first it was hard to talk, but the owner came over and told the teenagers to hold the noise down. When the ruckus stopped, she expressed her concerns about her farm. "I've been calling my mom all day. I think she's avoiding me."

"Why would she avoid you?"

She sipped her drink. "Laura has never been the most straightforward person. She beats around the bush about things and expects you to figure stuff out yourself. It drives me nuts."

"You told me earlier that she was your stepmother. You two must be pretty close if you call her Mom."

Emily nodded. "Sometimes I call her Mom. We're kind of close. My dad married Laura ten years ago, right before I graduated from high school." She shook her head, not wanting to discuss the somewhat complicated relationship she shared with her stepmother. "Believe me, I didn't start calling her Mom right away."

He opened his briefcase and removed a stack of paper before placing his reading glasses over his caramel eyes. She watched him flip through the papers, her curiosity about him sprouting like a geyser. He looked up and caught her staring. She looked away, wanting to put this whole situation into perspective. "What did you want to talk to me about?"

"Number one, I just want you to know that it's going to take me a long time, probably a week or more, to complete the audit for your farm. It'll be costly, but we have payment plans, and Laura has already signed the agreement."

"That figures," she mumbled. "She agrees to your services and doesn't tell me a thing."

He continued to flip through his papers. "I've

already accessed a great deal of your father's files, and I think I can help advise you and your mom about budgeting, forecasting, and doing the bookkeeping on your farm." He speared her with an intense look. "What I need from you is a description about where all of your revenue comes from. I know you get revenue from the milk, but where else do you get revenue? I just want to be sure your father has everything covered in all his files."

Emily started talking about where money flowed into their farm—from cows, beef cattle, heifers, and crops.

He interrupted her. "So, you have cash crops as well as crops you grow for feed?"

"We sure do. We've always done this, because it's hard to make a living from such a small herd of cows. We usually just plant extra so we'll have some left over to sell."

He continued to write, nodding. "I understand. A lot of smaller dairy farms must have some cash crops to survive."

"We hire outside help to assist with harvesting our crops."

He scanned his notes. "Are there any other sources of income?"

"No." She thought about it for a few seconds, figuring she had covered all of their revenue sources. Then she grabbed his arm. "Oh. I forgot about one thing. It's not a source of income directly from the farm, but it does help out."

Frank flipped to a fresh sheet of paper, encouraging her to continue. "Well, my mom's back went out on her a few years ago. So, bending over, milking the cows, and doing manual labor on the farm just wasn't agreeing with her anymore. Since she didn't work on the farm any longer for health reasons, she got a job down at the elementary school. She works in the cafeteria. She loves being around the kids, and she said the work isn't as intense as farming. Since the school is closed during the summer, she's free to do other things." Emily continued to talk nonstop about the farm for twenty minutes, and Frank took notes. She talked about her cows, telling him their names and describing their personalities.

"You name your cows? I've never seen a farmer do that."

"I don't name all of them, but I name my favorite ones." She explained that she had them trained to go into the same stall each night and that most of the larger farms didn't have such a personal relationship with their animals. Their pizza arrived, but she didn't touch it until she'd finished answering Frank's questions. He removed his reading glasses before he took the spatula and served thin slices of gooey, cheesy pizza onto the paper plates. She bowed her head, saying grace over her meal. Frank respectfully waited until she finished before he bit into his pizza.

She tasted her food, savoring the spices and the tangy pepperoni. "This is so good."

"Sure is." He took another healthy bite. After guzzling some of his soda, he focused on her again. "A lot of folks down my way like Chicago-style pizza. That's where I'm from."

"You're really from Chicago?"

He nodded, sipping his soda. "Yes, born and raised there. That's where my family lives." His cell phone buzzed. "Excuse me." He answered the call. "Hey, sport. Did you guys win the game?"

Frank's voice bellowed throughout the small restaurant. A few of the workers glanced in his direction. His grinned as he listened to the other person on the line. "Yes, I remember. What happened after you pitched?" The conversation continued for a few minutes. "Listen sport, I'm with a client now. I'll call you back tomorrow, okay?" He ended the call and set the phone onto the table.

"Was that your son?"

"No. That was my nephew, Mark." His smile faded as he stared at the pizza. He seemed to be thinking mighty hard about something. "My sister has two kids, and she's been having a rough time with them since her husband left her for another woman a year ago."

"That's awful." She couldn't imagine going through something like that. Having kids, taking care of them, and then for your spouse, the person who was supposed to be your partner, the most important person in the world, suddenly gone. It figured, a lot of the time, the mom had to raise the kids alone. A woman at her church had just gone through a nasty divorce. With two young children she'd been forced to return to a full-time job and the kids had been angry and bitter since their dad had left. "Does their dad ever see them?"

"A little. Not as much as he should. Emily, it's been pretty bad, so I made a point to spend a lot of time with the kids after their dad left." He shrugged as he took another slice of pizza. "I feel that every kid needs to have a dad, and I want to be there for them since their father doesn't seem to have time for them anymore."

Emily helped herself to another slice of pizza. "I think it's nice that you're helping your sister with her kids. I've seen so many single moms have to raise their kids alone." She shook her head. "That bothers me."

He sighed. "Yeah, it stinks." They ate in silence for a few minutes. "Hey, I wanted to ask you about something."

She wiped her hands on a napkin. "What's that?"

"I wanted to ask you about the posters on your wall. I noticed you have big pictures of the beach on your wall." He shrugged. "I like them. I was wondering if you like to travel."

She blew air through her lips. That'll be the day. "I've never traveled. Well…not outside of the immediate area."

He raised his eyebrows. "Really? You haven't traveled *anywhere*?" He shook his head. "I just can't imagine…" Well, it sounded like he didn't believe her. She glanced outside and eyed his Lexus. She figured he worked hard, was smart, and made a decent salary. She wondered if he'd been raised by wealthy parents, or, if he'd simply made a lot of money while working as an accountant. She didn't want to pry into his personal life, but, needed to be honest with him about hers.

"I love the beach, but the only beaches I've visited are Ocean City and Virginia Beach. I'd love to travel to one of those pretty blue beaches that I read about in travel magazines. I've been researching beaches online." She shrugged. "I've simply never had enough money to afford such a lavish vacation. I've dreamed about it enough. That's why I have those large posters on my walls." Well, that was enough information about her travel dreams. She highly doubted he'd want to hear her lament about not having enough money to visit her dream destinations. Maybe it was time to change the subject. She opened her purse and removed a foil wrapped square. She offered it to him. "Dessert?"

"Dessert?" He grinned as he stared at the foil packet, not accepting it. "What is that."

Well, he seemed a bit leery. She needed to put him at ease. She unwrapped it and the scent of rich chocolate escaped from the paper. She'd added plenty of roasted hazelnuts to her candy that morning so she was sure it would be delicious. "It's homemade milk chocolate candy."

"Homemade candy?"

She giggled. "Yes. I make milk chocolate candy." She shrugged. "I used raw cow's milk. Been doing this for years."

"Hmm…" He stared at the candy for a few seconds. "Are you sure that's safe to eat since the milk is unpasteurized?"

Heaven help her, she just couldn't resist. She giggled, then laughed. "It's fine. I'm sorry for laughing, you just looked so funny when I offered you the candy." She took a deep breath and calmed herself down. "It is dangerous to eat raw cow's milk. I pasteurize it before I use it. I heat it to a high temperature and let it cook for thirty minutes before I put it into my candy." She shrugged again. "Like I said, I've been doing this for a long time." He reached toward the candy, as if he were going to sample a piece. She touched his hand. "You're not allergic to nuts, are you?"

He shook his head. "No. I love nuts."

"Good." She tore a napkin from the dispenser, broke off a healthy piece of candy, placed it on the napkin, and then offered it to him. He accepted the candy and took a large bite. She focused on him, anxious to see his reaction. He took a tiny bite, chewed. He then took a large bite and grinned. "Tastes good. You used hazelnuts, didn't you?"

"Yes. Didn't you smell the chocolate while you were working today?"

He nodded as he helped himself to another

piece of candy. "Actually, I did. It smelled delicious."

He grinned as he continued eating her candy. Seeing him smile, his face lighting up, well…he just seemed more pleasant, nicer, than when they were talking in the office earlier. Maybe he'd been hungry earlier. He'd been grumpy. Far as she knew, he'd not stopped working to eat lunch. Laura had mentioned to her that men could get downright grumpy when they were hungry. Her curiosity about him sprouted like a geyser, and she wanted to know more about him. "So, how long have you lived in Maryland?"

"I've only been here a few days."

"Really?"

He nodded. He polished off another piece of candy before sipping his soda. "It was hard for me to leave my niece and nephew, but a lot has happened, Plus, my employer opened this new office and…well…if I do well, it could prove lucrative for me."

She leaned toward him. "Do you mean you'd get a raise?"

"Well…it's hard to say right now. I just need to wait and see what happens." He folded his arms. "I also moved here because I felt like I needed a change. Do you ever feel that way?"

She shook her head. "No, not really."

"Well, I did." He lifted his phone and glanced at the display for a few seconds before setting it back onto the table. "The accounting firm in the

Inner Harbor was expanding, and they opened the branch in Dairy to serve the farming community. Since they recently expanded into farm and ranch accounting, they needed somebody to temporarily head up that new division. One of the perks they offer to customers that many of the other farm and ranch accounting places don't offer is door-to-door service. That's why I came directly to your farm. Some accounting places require farmers to bring their files into their office or email them."

"So, you're only here temporarily?"

He shrugged. "I'm not sure. I didn't want to commit to stay long-term until I decided if I liked it here or not. Plus, as I said, I'm here to see how I perform in this new office. I also hope this job could lead to better things. I won't know for sure until later.

"Our main office in the Inner Harbor sometimes, too. I rented an apartment not far from the Inner Harbor."

"So, when they needed somebody, you volunteered?"

He shook his head. "Not initially. They came to me and asked me to do it, and I had to think about it for a bit before deciding to come. I had to get licensed to practice in the state of Maryland before I was able to make the move out here."

She frowned. Maybe he wasn't the right person to show them how to do their bookkeeping, especially since he just received his license in

Maryland. "What do you know about farm and ranch accounting since your company just recently started offering it to clients?"

"We have a farm and ranch division in Illinois. I advised a lot of farmers located in rural areas on the outskirts of Chicago. I'll admit you're the first client I've served via the door-to-door service. That's not something we offered in Illinois, but they're going to start offering that soon in that state also." He changed the subject. "You've always lived on your family's dairy farm?"

She nodded as she broke off another piece of candy. "I have one sister and two step-sisters. My sister, Sarah, hated farming. She left the farm when she was still in her early twenties. She lives in Idaho." She sipped her soda. "My stepsister Lisa lives in Florida, and Laura is visiting her right now. My other stepsister, Becky, is pregnant, and she lives in California. It's a difficult, high-risk pregnancy, and it's a shame she couldn't come to my father's funeral."

"Is this her first child?" Frank glanced at his phone again. His leg jiggled beneath the table. Was he nervous?

"No, she has two more, and she's really struggling right now. She's a stay- at-home mom, and her husband works full-time. Since her pregnancy has been so difficult and she is supposed to take it easy, a lot of people from her church have been helping her out."

"It sounds like you're close to your stepsisters."

Emily shook her head. "We're not really that close. I've seen them off and on since my dad married Laura. I'm not as close to them as I am to Sarah."

They ate in silence for a few minutes. She stifled a yawn. Maybe it was time to call it a night. She wanted to relax and read her Bible before going to bed. She was about to suggest he take her home, but, he looked directly at her, leaning closer. "Why are you so against your mother hiring an accountant? You never answered me earlier."

She sighed. Well, so much for leaving now. He'd probably ask her that question until she gave him an answer. Might as well tell him the truth. "This is a family business, and you are not family. When Dad died, I wanted to try and figure out the bookkeeping myself...." That was an understatement, she *had* tried to figure everything out, but, she'd failed miserably. And now...she was dependent on a stranger to look through their finances. She paused and gathered her thoughts. "I wanted my stepmother to help me to try and figure it out, but we kept arguing about it. I asked her if she'd at least wait for a couple of months to give me some time to go through Daddy's files."

"And she didn't agree to do that?" he guessed.

"I guess not, because she's gone and you're here."

"Well, your attitude is not very smart."

She narrowed her eyes and folded her arms in front of her chest. "I'm not stupid." No way did she want this man in their home, going through their finances, if he thought she were an idiot.

"I didn't say you were stupid." He took a deep breath. "I just meant that it's not very smart for you to do this on your own."

"What's wrong with that? It's *my* business."

He threw his hands into the air, as if he were tired of arguing with her. "I know it's your business. But, with a family business, it sometimes helps to get the opinion of an outsider."

She glanced around the restaurant. That uneasy feeling of having somebody in her house, looking through her father's files, niggled her. She eyed Frank. He was staring at her, but, he didn't look upset. *He wants to help me.* The thought slipped into her mind. Well, she'd still needed to hear him say why he'd said her actions were not very smart. "Why do you say that?"

He folded his arms in front of him, his leg continuing to jiggle. "Emily, you just admitted that you know nothing about the way your father accounted for the profits to your farm. You need an accountant to help you figure things out. You certainly don't want to be flagged for an audit by the IRS. If you are, it'll make things more difficult if you don't know what you're doing."

Pressing her lips together, she looked toward the counter. He touched her hand. "Hey, don't get offended. I just don't think you've thought through this very clearly."

"Whatever," she mumbled, draining her soda cup.

He chuckled, gazing at the empty pizza box. "I guess we had big appetites tonight."

"I tend to eat a lot of food."

"Do you?"

He seemed surprised, so she explained. "I've always eaten a lot of food, because doing those farm chores every day works up an appetite."

"You can't tell that you have a big appetite by looking at you," Frank said before he finished his soda.

Once he'd gathered his papers and placed them back into his briefcase, he closed it and paid the bill before they returned to his car. After he turned on the air conditioning, she rummaged through her purse. "I can pay for half the pizza."

"It's just a pizza. Besides, I can expense the meal since we were talking about business most of the time, anyway."

"I insist." She placed the money into his glove compartment.

"No, don't. Besides, you provided dessert. I loved your candy, by the way."

The way the compliment rolled from his mouth made her feel good. She took pride in her milk chocolate candy. Using the milk from her cows to make something sweet and delicious and enjoyable for folks caused her to have an even closer bond to her cows and to the family farm. Her skin heated with pleasure as she popped open the glove compartment and reclaimed her money. She shoved the folded bills back into her purse. "Thank you."

"You're welcome." When they pulled into the dairy farm, he leaned out the window as soon as she'd rushed from the car. "Remember, I'll be back tomorrow. Is nine o'clock okay?"

"That's fine."

She stood in the driveway and took a deep breath. She glanced up. Stars dotted the dark sky and a smooth gentle breeze blew. The leaves on the trees whispered in the wind. It felt so nice. She needed to sit out on the porch and enjoy this nice evening.

After lighting some citronella candles, she plopped into a chair and removed her phone from her purse. She accessed the Tahitian websites that she visited regularly, admiring the beautiful beaches. She could just sit and stare at these pictures all day. Her love for beaches had sort of started when she'd first learned to swim. When she was only four, her mom had still been alive, and she'd taken her for her first swimming lessons at the YMCA. Her mom had braided her hair into tight cornrows and had gotten her a snug swimming cap, wanting to be sure her hair didn't get wet with the chlorinated water.

She'd loved it.

She swam regularly, begging her mom to take

her to the pool whenever she had time and wasn't busy on the farm. She'd been active on her high school swim team and had continued swimming through college. Her love for swimming expanded from swimming pool to beaches. As an adult, she'd visited her cousin Monica in Ocean City. During her short visits, she'd loved swimming in the Atlantic Ocean. She'd visited Jamaica and the Bahamas with her church on mission trips. She'd loved sharing her faith with others, and during those mission trips, she'd had a wonderful time swimming in the pretty water.

She'd made a project out of studying about different beaches. She'd been mesmerized by the beautiful beaches around the world, but, there was just something about Tahiti that tugged her. She wanted to go, so bad.

By the candlelight, she flipped scrolled through the beautiful pictures of Tahitian scenery on her phone. She loved looking at the beautiful beaches, the sting rays, the fish. *Lord, this looks so beautiful.* She then accessed her private savings account. She'd started saving for her Tahitian trip over a year ago.

It would take her a long time to save up for a such a luxurious trip on a measly farmer's salary. Hopefully, she'd have enough money saved up in a few years. Her phone buzzed – a text from her best friend, Kelly.

Hey, getting ready to call you.

She couldn't talk, not now. *Not tonight. Too tired.*

As briefly as she could, she texted about Laura hiring Frank.

Kelly texted back with a sad face emoticon. *Why don't all three of us go out for lunch this weekend to cheer you up?*

The threesome included Emily, Christine and Kelly. She smiled. Maybe some girl time was just what she needed.

She texted back. *Great. Will call tomorrow.*

Her phone buzzed.

Laura.

Lord, please help me with my anger. She gripped the phone and slowly counted to ten. She hated that Laura had hired Frank without getting her consent beforehand. "Why did you hire that accountant without asking me first?"

CHAPTER 3

FOLLOWING THE FORTY-MINUTE drive from Dairy, Frank cruised down Pratt Street near the Inner Harbor. He barely paid attention to the throngs of people walking the sidewalks on the warm summer night. The blue electric wave decorating the Baltimore Aquarium blazed in the darkness, and he sighed, anxious to get to his recently rented apartment in the heart of Baltimore.

Once he'd parked, he opened the door to his backseat and removed the glass bottles filled with liquor. He sighed, riding the elevator to his loft apartment. After unlocking the door, he threw his briefcase onto the couch, opened the refrigerator, and pulled out a club soda. He placed several ice cubes into the plastic tumbler. He then poured a little soda over the ice before pouring a healthy amount of his favorite imported scotch into the container. Sitting on the couch, he sipped his drink, his frazzled nerves slowly calming after he'd drunk half the amount in the glass.

The nervous twitch in his leg stopped when he settled into his nighttime routine. He lifted the remote, turning on the network news, thinking about his weird day. When his boss suggested he take the Cooper client, he felt it was just what he needed.

He wasn't sure how he felt about his working at the farm.

Emily was strange…Cute, but strange. She'd had the strongest reaction when she'd spotted his booze. There was nothing wrong with having a good stiff drink. Earlier, while he'd been working in her father's office, he'd noticed a Bible and a book of devotionals on the shelf. Folks drank wine in the Bible, so, it wasn't like it was wrong or anything. She'd prayed before eating her dinner…lots of folks prayed before eating. He wondered if she were a church girl who didn't *do* anything. He picked up on her strong work ethic right away. Plus, she'd seemed honest. He couldn't believe she'd insisted on paying for half of a pizza after he'd said he'd expense the meal.

He shook his head as he continued to nurse his drink. With her dad dying, it must be rough for her and her stepmom running that farm alone.

He shook his head. Emily reminded him so much of his dead wife Julie that it was scary. He got up returned to the kitchen and fixed another drink. When he returned to the couch, he lifted his wedding photo, touching Julie's face. He squeezed his eyes shut. When would it stop hurting? He took several deep breaths and kissed his wife's photo. Taking sip after sip, his mind grew fuzzy as the alcohol chased away the demons that haunted him.

During the next few days working on Emily's farm, Frank worked hard on the going through the accounting ledgers for Emily's farm. She patiently answered his questions about the farm, providing necessary information he needed to do his job. They called her stepmother via speakerphone, and he consulted with Laura about what he planned on doing about the bookkeeping and the audit. He told the older woman he'd be doing the audit for at least a week or more, and she seemed to accept his presence in her home.

When Frank struggled to open his eyes the following Saturday morning, his head felt like it was going to explode. He eyed the clock beside his bed. Six thirty. Once he drank a few cups of black coffee, he would feel ready to go into the office before heading out to Emily's farm. His boss was always hounding him about working too many overtime hours on the weekends, but Frank found he enjoyed working more than being alone in his apartment. Working long hours helped make his mind too tired to dwell on the problems he struggled to forget.

Besides, he needed to continue to work these

long hours to prove what a great addition he'd be as partner. If he were made partner, he could use that money to—His phone buzzed. He glanced at the caller ID.

His sister Trish. He groaned. He closed his eyes and sighed for a few seconds before answering the call. "What is it, Trish?"

"Good morning to you, too, little brother. I should have had Mark call you from his phone instead. You seem happier talking to my children than to me."

He lay back on the pillow, trying to relieve his throbbing headache, ignoring her apt observation. "Do you realize it's six thirty in the morning?"

"Yes, but I've been calling you since you moved to Baltimore, and you never answer your phone, yet you always answer when Mark calls. I figured if I called you early enough, you'd at least think it was an emergency."

He rubbed his eyes. "Is there an emergency?"

She hesitated. "Yes."

Trish was known for stretching the truth. If there was really an emergency, she would've already told him about it. "What's wrong?"

"Mom's been pretty upset since you left."

"I've been pretty upset since she rejected my wife." His sister sighed as he gripped the phone. What did Trish expect? Most people would be angry if their parents treated their spouse the way they'd treated Julie, wouldn't they? "What does Mom want me to do?"

"She wants you to start talking to her and Dad again. Julie is no longer with us and—"

"Just because Julie died, that means I need to forget what they've done?" What kind of logic was that? Being around his parents just reminded him about how they'd treated Julie. It made him sick, literally, and he honestly didn't know when he could stomach being around his parents again. He squeezed his eyes shut. Memories of his dad showing him to ride a bike rushed through his mind. He'd been about five and his dad had removed the training wheels and had promised to hold onto the back of the seat until Frank had learned to balance himself. It'd been one long, hot afternoon but, at the end of the day, he'd learned to ride. The thrill of rushing down that hill, pedaling hard, the wind gushing around him. When he'd returned to their house his dad had hugged him, hard.

Thinking about the fun he'd had as a kid with both of his parents – then thinking how they'd treated Julie – the memories from both extremes played an internal war, deep in his gut, a war that seemed to go on forever. It exhausted him, made him want to go back into his bed and cover his head with a huge blanket and then fall asleep. At least if he were asleep, he could forget about all that was bothering him, unless he dreamed about it. There seemed to be no escaping these thoughts, except through alcohol and work.

"Frank, it's been over a year. Don't you think it's time to move on?"

Could he move on? Could he do that knowing how his parents felt about Julie?

"I just don't know, Julie." He massaged his forehead. "Look, my head hurts, and I don't feel like talking about this right now."

She ignored his comment. "Dad hasn't been feeling well."

He sat up in bed, his stomach churning from the sudden movement. He took a few deep breaths. "Is he okay?"

"See, I know you still care."

He ignored the comment. "Is Dad okay?"

"He's been complaining a lot about having a headache, and Mom says he's hardly eating."

"What does the doctor say?"

She sighed, her voice wavering. "He refuses to go to the doctor." The sib- lings were silent for a few seconds before Trish spoke again. "I think Dad's guilt about what happened is eating away at him."

That figured. He closed his eyes. "Trish, you know they were wrong. You finally became friends with Julie. You know how much I loved her. You know why I loved her."

"I loved Julie, too."

"I know you did. She always told me if she were to have a sister, she'd want her to be just like you."

"I know. That's why you really need to get

over yourself and stop running away from your problems."

"I'm not running away—"

"But you are. Don't you get it?"

"No, I don't know what you're talking about."

"Yes, you do. I'll bet you're still having nightmares about Julie's death, and you probably have a headache because you got drunk last night."

Frank winced. "I'm dealing with it the only way I know."

"Well, you need to find another way to deal with your pain. Alcohol and nightmares are doing nothing to help you."

"Well, what do you suggest?" It'd be interesting to hear what she had to say.

"If I told you, you wouldn't want to hear it."

"Try."

"Why don't you do what Julie would have wanted you to do? Why don't you give God a chance? Since Julie led me to the Lord, I've found it so much easier to deal with my problems."

"I don't see how you can talk about trusting the Lord. Your husband left you. Look at all the problems you've been having with Mark and Regina since he left."

"It's been hard, but I'm trying to teach my kids that even though their earthly father is not around much anymore, they have a heavenly Father who loves them and will never leave them." Faith was a personal thing and he just didn't have any. Not now. It was useless to try and argue with Julie, so, he didn't say a word. "You might want to give God a try and let Him help you with all that you're dealing with. Another thing you might want to do is not be so angry at Mom and Dad."

"Wait a minute."

"No, you wait a minute. Just hear me out about this. I know Mom and Dad didn't like Julie because she didn't come from a good family, and it was wrong of them to think like that. But you have to remember that money's been in our family for decades, and Mom and Dad have been raised to think this way. It's wrong, but in their own twisted way, they felt this was one way to show their love for us: making sure we chose an appropriate mate from a prestigious family."

Before he could say anything, she changed the subject. "You'll never guess who I saw at the grocery store yesterday."

"Who?"

"Brian. He said a lot of the kids at the rec center still ask about you, and I told him that you'd moved to Baltimore." She sighed. "You've been so sad and bitter since Julie died. You used to be so happy spending your free time at the rec center helping Brian mentor those teenagers. I remember how you used to look forward to having some kids of your own."

He swiped the sudden tears from his eyes. He didn't want to tell Trish about his hope for getting the partnership. Hearing her talk about

Brian made him remember what he'd planned on doing with some of the extra money he might be making from the partnership – if he were made partner.

Thoughts of playing basketball at the rec center filled his mind. Those kids – he'd been a mentor, someone they could look up to. He'd thrived on spending his free time with the teenaged boys… it'd been fun. He recalled the names of the boys he'd mentored and did a quick calculation – they'd be over a year older – young people grew so fast…the urge to see them again. Maybe he should visit Chicago soon and stop through the rec center for a quick visit.

"Look, I have to go now. I need to start making breakfast for the kids. I just wanted you to think about what I've told you and to try and talk to Mom and Dad again."

He wiped his eyes and grunted before he ended the call. He finally sat up popped took some Tylenol. His stomach roiled as he made his way to the kitchen. He measured dark grinds into the filter, and the fragrant scent of coffee soon filled the air. Taking a mug from the cupboard, he filled it with his morning brew, sat at a chair in the kitchen, and thought about Trish's advice. He just wasn't ready to forgive his parents for what they'd done—he just couldn't.

A few hours later he dressed and called Emily. He was surprised when she answered on the first ring. "Hi, I thought you would be out milking the cows."

"I'm finished with that already. I do it at 5:00 a.m."

He chuckled. "Actually, I was awake at six thirty this morning."

"Really?"

He sensed she was going to say something else, but when she remained silent, he continued. "Look, I know it's Saturday, but I wanted to know if it was okay if I came to your farm for a few hours today. I need to go to the auction—"

"You're going to the auction over in Westminster?"

"Yes, I was going to head over there because my boss said it was a good idea to see what the livestock are selling for. I agreed to go, so after I do that, I thought I could spend a few hours on your father's files."

"Could I ask a huge favor of you?"

"What's up?"

"Could you pick me up for the auction? My truck is still in the shop, and I didn't want to spend money on a rental. I borrowed a truck from another farmer for a few days to run some errands, but the garage said my vehicle is still not fixed."

"I don't mind picking you up. Are you planning on adding to your herd?"

"No, I'm going for another reason. I'll explain when you get here."

"Okay. See you soon."

A few minutes later he exited his apartment building and stopped as a woman walked by. The ivory suit and high heels reminded him of one of Julie's favorite outfits. The female had a surety to her step as she sauntered by, and Frank felt frozen in time when he watched her.

The woman's dark eyes widened as he stared. "I'm sorry, I thought you were somebody else." he explained, ashamed to be caught staring at a woman who resembled his wife. She frowned and walked away. Frank leaned against his apartment building, the bright sun shining in his eyes. That was the third time since Julie's death that he'd made this error. He closed his eyes, wondering when he'd learn to accept that his wife was dead and move on with his life.

He shook his head, strolling to the small parking lot. Once he got into his vehicle, he stared out the window. Maybe spending the day with Emily at an auction was what he needed to get his mind off his nightmares.

Yawning, Emily tried to relax the kink in her shoulders before she pulled on the sundress and slid her feet into her comfortable sandals. She yawned again as she trudged into the kitchen. She needed to be sure she was ready before Frank arrived to take her to the auction.

If she didn't have plans for the auction, she would've taken a nap. She was in the middle of stifling another yawn when a hard knock at the door jolted her awake. Good thing Frank was here. She just remembered something she wanted to talk to him about and she didn't want to forget later. She opened the door.

Cameron. She didn't feel like talking to him… or attempting to talk to him. Cam stuttered. It was difficult to hold a conversation with him – she had to be polite, but, she needed to be patient and really focus on him while he spoke. She had to give him ample time to say what was on his mind before she could respond. She cleared her throat eyed the milk truck driver. "Good morning, Cam."

"H-h-h-i, E-Emily." Without asking, he removed his hat and slowly strolled into the kitchen. "I've already put your m-m-milk in the t-tank. I just stopped in to say h-hello."

She tried to smile. No way was she going to encourage him by saying it was fine that he'd stopped by.

"You look r-real n-nice this m-morning." He crumpled his baseball cap between his thick, dark fingers.

"Thanks Cam. I was just about to have a glass of water. Did you want some?"

"No, t-thanks."

Cameron studied her while she poured the glass of water.

She gulped her beverage before placing the glass in the sink.

He grabbed the back of a chair and pulled it away from the table. Gesturing toward the seat. "You l-look like you could use a r-rest."

His hands trembled. Good grief, he looked scared – as if she were going to reach over and force him out the door. He'd probably find himself a girlfriend in no time if he weren't so nervous around women. He wasn't a bad-looking man, but he hovered, clearly making his interest in her known. This had been going on for some time and she honestly didn't have a clue as to how to get him to accept that she wasn't interested in spending time with him. She gave him a quick glance as she poured her coffee. Tall and stocky with thick muscled arms and dark cocoa brown skin…if he wasn't so nervous, and didn't stutter, she could imagine a host of eligible women flocking to the milk truck driver.

Emily poured a cup of coffee and sat in the offered chair. "Would you like some coffee?" He had a schedule to keep, so, she figured he'd refuse. She just offered to be polite.

He shook his head. "No t-thanks. I'm going to be l-leaving soon anyway." He frowned. "You look tired. Is something w-wrong?"

She clutched the coffee mug, closing her eyes briefly. "No, nothing's wrong." She took another sip of coffee. "I don't mean to keep you from getting to your next milk pickup." Hopefully he'd leave before Frank arrived.

She glanced at the screen door.

Frank. Thank God he'd arrived. Now maybe Cam would leave. She didn't want to make him late for his next scheduled pickup. "Frank, come on in." Her throat was suddenly dry. She sipped from her mug of coffee as Frank entered the kitchen. The cool scent of his aftershave filled the room with musky sweetness.

Frank focused on Cam and offered his hand. "I'm Frank."

"C-C-Cam. I'm in charge of the m-milk p-pick up."

Frank nodded and lo and behold, he started talking to Cam. Cam's stutter didn't seem to bother Frank as he asked Cam about milk prices, his job, how he'd come to be a milk pickup man. Cam stood a bit taller and she realized his stutter wasn't so thick when he realized that Frank's interest seemed genuine.

Frank. She'd gotten to know him during the past week. He'd told her that his nephew called him every day, saying he wished Frank had not left. He regretted missing Mark's Little League games, and since he'd left, his sister, Trish, said that Mark had started misbehaving again. Frank had mentioned that he planned to take a weekend and visit Trish and her children soon and that he was still angry that Trish's husband had abandoned their family a year ago.

"Let me give you my number. Maybe we can catch an Orioles game sometime." Now the two men were talking about sports. Cam was a loner and she'd always assumed he preferred it that way. Cam grinned as they exchanged phone numbers.

Compassionate. Frank cared. She sensed that he figured that Cam probably had few friends because of his stutter and Frank wanted to make everything better. Frank cared about people – just as he cared about his family. Whenever he spoke of his niece and nephew, his face brightened, and when Mark called, Frank dropped what he was doing to see what his nephew wanted to talk about.

She'd been working closely with Frank this week as they went over her father's accounting records. Whenever he looked at her, she became flustered, her heart racing like a horse speeding out to pasture. She couldn't seem to keep Frank from dominating her thoughts—or tempting her heart.

"W-well. I'd better get g-going." Cam shook hands with Frank and nodded toward Emily. "I'll see you in a couple of d-days, E-Emily." The screen door banged shut when he left.

"Morning, Emily."

"Morning, Frank." She gestured toward the screen door. "It was nice of you to talk to Cam."

Frank made himself comfortable in a chair. "Yeah." He eyed her, grinning. "He have a crush on you?" He chuckled. "I noticed him staring at you when I came to the door."

She didn't feel like talking about Cam. Frank looked nice in his t-shirt and jeans. Wow, spending the day with him outside of the farm…well… she was looking forward to it. She frowned. Why were his eyes so red? Did he have allergies? He rubbed his stomach as if it hurt. Maybe it wasn't a good idea to spend the day with him. Whatever illness he had she certainly didn't want to catch it. She tapped his shoulder. "Hey, you feeling okay?"

"Yeah. Why?"

"Your eyes are red. Maybe you have allergies. Lots of folks around here have them during the summer. It's possible that you're allergic to some plants around here that you're not exposed to in Chicago."

"No, I don't have allergies."

"Well what's wrong?"

He narrowed his eyes. "Nothing. You ready to go?"

Okay, he didn't want to talk about how he was feeling. Well, she'd respect that. Maybe he'd feel more comfortable about it and confide to her later. He could be worried about something and had trouble sleeping. She knew firsthand how hard it could be to sleep when you had something on your mind.

"Coffee?" She gestured toward the pot.

"No thanks."

"I have to eat first." She went to the cupboard

to get a box of cereal. She poured cornflakes into a large bowl then gestured toward the box. "Did you want some cereal?"

He shook his head and touched his stomach. "I don't want any breakfast this morning."

She peered at him again, and he squirmed beneath her intense gaze. "Does your stomach hurt every morning?"

He sighed, scooting his chair back. "I don't feel well this morning."

He didn't answer her question. Well, she couldn't force him to talk. She let the subject drop, adding milk and banana to her cereal. She prayed over her meal. She then dipped her spoon into the bowl and enjoyed her simple meal.

"So, why are you going to the auction today if you're not planning on purchasing any cows?"

In between large bites of cereal, she explained. "My father and I used to go to the auction as a social outlet. We'd talk to other farmers, look at the animals being auctioned off—that sort of thing. Sometimes we'd sell our beef cattle there, but I don't have one that's old enough to sell right now." She stopped eating. "We'd already planned to go today. . .before he passed. And I just want to go because I like going."

When she finished her cereal, she drank the last of the milk from the bowl, and Frank chuckled. "That's the biggest bowl of cereal I've ever seen a woman eat."

She grinned. "I told you milking those cows every morning and doing chores makes me work up an appetite."

"Did your farm help come this morning?"

She nodded as she rinsed out her cereal bowl and placed it in the dishwasher. "Yes, one of them showed up. They've been doing pretty good since Casey had her calf." When she was finished in the kitchen, she went to her bedroom to get her purse. "Are you ready to go?" She removed her housekeys from her handbag. Frank nodded as she locked the door before they headed to his vehicle.

After they were settled in his car, he turned the air conditioning up as he pulled away from the house. "You'll need to tell me where to go unless you want me to use the GPS on my phone."

"I don't mind giving you directions." She settled into the leather seat. Man, this air conditioning sure felt good. Maybe she should use some of her savings to get the AC fixed on her truck.

"Do you know when they're going to get your truck repaired?"

"They had to order some parts. It shouldn't be too much longer before it's fixed. Probably next week sometime." When he stopped at a light, he removed a pair of shades from his glove compartment. He placed his sunglasses over his eyes. "Did your mom ever tell you why she hired me without asking you first?"

Emily sighed, folding her arms in front of her. "Yes. She knew that I'd never agree and she figured she was doing the right thing."

He glanced at her before pulling away from the light. "Do you believe her?"

She shrugged. "I don't know. My stepmother is certainly not prone to lying. She does seem to overstep her boundaries sometimes, though. This should have been a decision we made together." She looked out the window, frowning. "Since my daddy died, I don't know what to believe anymore."

"What do you mean?"

"Nothing is the same. You know, when somebody you love is alive, you just take the days for granted, thinking you'll see them the next day. Now that my daddy's dead, my stepmother hasn't been the same—I haven't been the same. I can't sleep, she can't sleep, and the only solace I seem to find is working with the cows and reading my Bible."

"If God is so almighty, then why does He allow people to suffer so much?"

Why was he asking this now? Well, she didn't want to pry. All she could do was answer the question the best that she could. "I don't know, but my belief in Him and knowing my dad is in heaven gives me some comfort."

He changed the subject. "Is that all your mother said?"

"Pretty much. I've spoken to her a few times

since you've started the audit. Ever since she's been in Florida with her daughter, she sounds happier. I almost feel like she doesn't want to come home."

"Do you still think she's only going to stay for a few weeks?"

"It's hard to say. The elementary school is closed for the summer, so I guess she's not in a hurry to come home."

"I see. Is that all she said?"

She watched him carefully. "Is there something wrong?"

Tension knotted her muscles when she noticed he clutched the steering wheel. "It's still early in the audit process. Your father's budget looks good, but I can't tell you about the financial solvency of your farm until I've completed the audit." He sighed when he stopped at another light. "I just found out something interesting yesterday that I thought you should know. I figured your mom would've told you when she called, but she obviously didn't."

"What are you talking about?"

The car behind them honked, prompting them to drive since the light had changed. He quickly turned left onto Highway 137. "I was looking through your father's computer files, and I found a spreadsheet that he called Estimated Selling Cost. I also found some correspondence he had with a Realtor."

"A Realtor? What Realtor?"

Frank shrugged. "There wasn't a name or address, but it looked like he was drafting an e-mail to a property salesman. The spreadsheet listed properties that were recently sold in the Baltimore County area that were similar to your farm."

"Why would my dad be in contact with a Realtor?"

He shrugged. "It's hard to say, but from looking at the files, it appears as if he was thinking about selling your property."

That didn't sound right. "Are you sure?"

He kept one hand on the steering wheel and touched her arm with the other. He shook his head. "No, I'm not sure. I'm only speculating. I can show you what I found if you'd like."

Whoa, this was a lot to process. Was her dad really planning to sell the farm without telling her about it? That was low-handed and awful. She pressed her hands together. She couldn't even speak. Her dad wasn't like that. He was always open and honest, especially about the farm. The two of them were a team, always had been. They'd shared a deep bond for farming that didn't spill over to her sister Sarah and her stepmom.

He touched her hand. "Are you okay?" He squeezed her hand. The concern in his deep voice trilled from her head right down to her toes. He'd pulled over to a fast food restaurant and stopped the car, as if he sensed she needed a minute. "Did you want me to give you a few minutes alone?" *He cares. He doesn't want me to feel hurt.*

She shook her head and removed her hand from his. She already missed the warmth from his gentle touch. "Look, we need to get going. I don't want to make us late."

He simply nodded before they returned to the main road.

She took several deep breaths. "I can't believe my dad would even think about selling our farm."

"He might not have been trying to sell. I'm only speculating. Besides, he may have wanted to tell you about his intentions…well…before he passed."

She took a few deep breaths. Maybe some time alone was what she needed. But, she didn't need a few minutes, more like a few hours. They were already on their way to the auction, so, no sense in ruining their visit. Maybe being at the auction would help take her mind off of everything. She breathed deeply. She needed to calm down before they arrived at the auction.

He glanced in her direction. "Where do I turn?" They'd entered a roundabout.

"Make a right at the first road."

He took the first exit. The information about her father sat in her brain like a twisted knot, waiting to be untangled. She definitely needed to speak with her stepmother again.

She watched the passing scenery. "I don't understand why Laura didn't tell me all this."

"Maybe she didn't know. Are sure you're okay?"

"No, I'm upset." Her life suddenly seemed to be speeding out of control, and she wondered what other secrets her father may have been harboring. *Jesus, I really need your help right now.*

CHAPTER 4

WHEN THE LIVESTOCK auction was finished, people cleared out of the enclosure. Frank touched her elbow as they strolled to his car. During the auction he'd been keeping his eye on her.

She'd left a few times to go to the ladies' room. He figured she'd been upset. Maybe he should've insisted that they go to another auction later, when she was feeling better. They'd had a light lunch, just hot dogs, during the auction. It was almost dinnertime so, he figured good hot meal was what she needed to make her feel better. "I guess you need to be getting home to milk the cows?"

"Both of the brothers are supposed to come tonight for the milking."

"Did you want to get a bite to eat? I know how much you hate cooking." He opened her door for her, and they settled into his vehicle.

She bit her lower lip, staring out the windshield. "Frank, I don't know—"

"I wanted to talk to you about something."

"Can't we talk about it now?"

"Well, you're hungry, aren't you?"

She nodded, and smiled. She looked so downright cute and sexy when she smiled. She had the cutest dimple on her cheek and her lips….what would happen if he leaned over and kissed her right now? He wished there were a way that he could erase the news about her day and just start over – that way, the cloud of sadness wouldn't be hovering over her like an unwelcome rain storm.

"Of course, I'm hungry."

"Then let's get something to eat."

"Okay. Let me call Jeremy and Darren to make sure they're doing the milking right now." Once she called and confirmed that both brothers had shown up at her farm and were milking the cows, he drove them downtown to the Inner Harbor in Baltimore. After he parked in a garage, they entered the trendy tourist district. "Do you want to eat at The Cheesecake Factory?"

She nodded as they approached the high-class restaurant. Noise filtered from the dining crowd. When they approached the hostess, she gave them a pager and placed their names on a list. "There's an hour wait." The petite attractive hostess spoke loudly above the noise. "We'll page you when the table is ready. Just be sure you don't go too far away."

Emily gestured toward the pager. "So, a whole hour?" He agreed with her. That was an awfully long time to wait when you were hungry.

The hostess shrugged. "We're always busy on Saturday evenings."

Frank accepted the pager. They strolled around the Inner Harbor. The breeze blew over the water. "Come sit with me for a minute?" He nodded toward a bench.

She made herself comfortable on the seat beside him. Boats bobbed on the Chesapeake Bay, and throngs of people walked by, many carrying bags of purchases from the shops in Harborplace. A jazz saxophonist played his horn, and several people dropped money into his instrument case. The music surrounded them, the mellow notes filling the air.

She tilted her head back, closing her eyes. "It sure is nice out here." The hot wind blew her ponytail. Frank eyed the guys who strolled nearby.

Some of them gave Emily a second look.

Emily leaned back her eyes closed. Her sandaled foot tapped to the tune of the saxophone player. What would happen if he put his arm around her? Would she get mad? Well, he wouldn't take that chance, not now anyway.

"Yes, it is nice. Do you come here often?"

She shook her head. "Not much. Sometimes my friends and I come out here for dinner. But we haven't done that in months."

They sat in companionable silence. The red lights on the pager brightened when the instrument buzzed. "I guess our table is ready."

Her stomach growled. Their server approached. "My name is Allen, and I'll be your server tonight. What can I get you all to drink?"

Frank's leg was twitching. What was up with that? Was he nervous about something? He was a hard worker, maybe he felt guilty about taking the day off to go to the auction.

Frank cleared his throat. "I'll have a Coke."

"I'll have lemonade and a glass of water."

Allen soon reappeared with their drinks. "I'm ready for your food orders."

Great, she needed some food. "I'll have the Cajun jambalaya pasta."

"Jamaican black pepper shrimp." Frank shut his menu and returned it to Allen. After their waiter had left, she focused on Frank. He sure was easy on the eyes. His strong jaw, long lashes…full lips made for kissing. He gulped his Coke and stopped as soon as he caught her staring.

Could this be more embarrassing? Well, she didn't need him to know what she'd been thinking. The last think she needed to be thinking about was kissing a man when the future of her dairy farm seemed at stake.

He grinned and winked at her, quick as could be. Was he flirting? Her skin heated. He laughed, the loud bellow causing others to look in their direction. "Emily, you are too funny." "What?"

He chuckled. "People can be attracted to each other. Its okay." He chuckled again. "I'm sure you've had boyfriends over the years. If I didn't know better, I'd think you were a virgin or something."

Whoa, that was totally inappropriate. What if somebody heard that? They were at a public place, not at her house. His smile faded and he looked directly at her. "Are you seriously…." He didn't finish the sentence.

"Yes, I *am*…seriously." What a sensitive topic to discuss at a public dinner table. Frank should've had better manners.

He set his glass down and took her hand. "Hey, I'm sorry." His deep voice lowered with concern as he looked directly into her eyes. "I shouldn't have said that. I'm sorry."

She nodded and removed her hand. "Apology accepted."

"You've never dated at all?" Well, sounded like he didn't believe her.

"Yes, I've dated." She didn't want to talk about that right now. She needed to figure out what had been going on with her dad and she needed Frank's help. "Do you really think my father would want to sell his farm?"

He looked at her, frowning. "Are you sure you

don't want to talk to your stepmother about this some more?" He sipped his soda.

She took a drink of water. "I guess I should. Mom's hiding something. I can feel it."

He sighed. "Like I said earlier, it looks as if your dad may have been planning to sell, but I can't tell for sure."

"Sweetheart, don't worry about this until you talk to Laura."

The endearment rolled off his tongue and settled into her heart. She ignored the feeling, again focusing on the news he'd delivered. "Well, you're wrong. My dad would not sell the farm. I've never met a person who loved dairy farming more than Paul Cooper. Plus, my dad inherited our farm from his father. My grandfather was one of the first African American dairy farmers in Baltimore County. Dairy farming is in our blood, and I can't imagine my father giving that up."

He quickly squeezed her hand. "You're probably right. You seem to know your dad pretty well. He may have been contacting a Realtor for a different reason."

A horrible thought occurred to her. "Do you think my stepmother wants to sell, and she just hasn't told me?" The thought sickened her. When her plate of jambalaya arrived, she pushed it away. She'd lost her appetite. Maybe she could get the food in a to-go box.

Frank massaged her fingers. "Are you sure you're okay?"

She glanced down at their hands. She didn't have the energy to pull away and there was something comforting in the way he was touching her hand. She finally pulled her hand away. Maybe going out to dinner wasn't such a good idea after all. "You didn't answer my question."

He sampled his shrimp. "I honestly don't know. Maybe you should call your stepmom tonight and talk to her about everything."

"Yeah, I just might." She stared at her food. She wanted to go home, take a long bath, and put on her comfortable robe and slippers. After relaxing a bit, she'd then call her stepmom. As he ate, she prayed before she sampled her meal. Although her food tasted good, she only ate a few bites. Once Frank had finished all of the food on his plate, he took a look at her plate.

"Mind if I have a taste?" He grinned and gave her another quick wink.

Chuckling she took a clean spoon and scooped some of her food onto his plate. She made sure she gave him some from the side of the plate which she'd not eaten. "This is delicious. I'm going to get this the next time we come here."

The next time they came? He acted as if they'd be making a habit of coming here. Sure, he'd held her hand, and had been concerned about her. Sure, she'd been daydreaming about kissing him…but, she didn't think they'd be going out on a *real* date. She had so much going on with her farm. After he was done with the audit, would he still return to visit her? Could she be bold enough to get in her pickup truck and visit him at his apartment?

After he'd finished eating, Emily requested a take-out box for her leftovers.

Afterward they walked around Harborplace before they returned to Frank's car. He drove her home and cut off the ignition when they arrived at her farm. "Do you mind if we sit on your porch?"

Hmmm….the thought of sitting with Frank on the porch on a star-filled night…delicious warmth spread in stomach. "Sure. Sounds like a good idea."

They walked to the porch and sat on the swing. "You got any of that candy you make?"

"No, I'd planned on making some soon. I'll be sure to put some aside for you."

"Thanks. Are you sure you're okay?"

She nodded. "I'm fine. I just don't know what kinds of things my step- mother is hiding." She looked at him. "I also don't like what you told me about my dad. I feel like I'm being lied to."

He sighed. "Emily. . ."

She shook her head. "I guess you'll be back next week to continue working in my dad's office?"

"Yes, I'll be back next week. I'm not sure what time, though, because I have some meetings to attend." Crickets chirped in the hot summer air. Emily's stomach flipped when Frank held her hand. Sparks of warmth shot up her arm. "Can I ask you something?"

She looked at him. "What?"

"I really had a good time tonight. I also enjoyed having dinner with you at Leonardo's."

She smiled, her belly curling with warmth. "Yeah, I had a good time, too."

"I wondered if you wanted to get together again sometime next week. Maybe we can go to a movie or something." He squeezed her hand. "I like spending time with you, and I want to get to know you better."

She pulled her hand away. "I'll be honest with you. I like spending time with you, too, but there are things about you that bother me."

"What kinds of things?"

"When we went to Leonardo's, I saw the liquor bottles in your car."

He grunted. "I know, we talked about that. It's no big deal."

The swing rocked. She needed to be sure she said this properly. She didn't want to offend him, but, there were things about him that she needed to know before she agreed to their seeing one another again. "Do you drink every day?"

"Yes."

"Why?"

He threw his hands up in the air, frowning. "Why is it such a big deal? Why are you asking?"

"You just asked about us going out. These are things I need to know about somebody before I agree to a date."

He sighed. "When something heavy is on my

mind, I drink to forget. I've been doing this for about a year now. I've had problems with it before that, but I was able to quit eventually."

"What's on your mind?"

"It's kind of complicated. My parents did some awful things, and I can't let my anger go."

Letting go of anger could be challenging. Although it could be hard, it was usually the only way to find peace. "You really need to forgive your parents. If their actions make you drink, then you need to do something else to deal with your pain."

"I'm almost afraid to ask what you would do if you were me."

Well, he asked. She wasn't sure how he'd react to her response. Since they didn't know one another very well, it probably wasn't clear about how she placed Jesus first in her life…at least she tried to do so. "Are you a Christian?"

"I believe in God."

She shook her head, looking at him. "I didn't ask if you believed in God. I asked if you're a Christian."

"I've noticed that a lot of people say they are Christians, but it doesn't necessarily mean the same thing to everybody."

He was avoiding her question. Maybe it would help if she were more direct. "When I use the term 'Christian,' I'm referring to somebody who has accepted Christ as their Savior and who trusts

Him completely. Can you honestly tell me you've done this?"

Well, he wasn't saying anything. That figured. She'd noticed it was hard for some people to talk about faith and God. Her friend Kelly told her that when she was at work people had to be careful about how they spoke to others – some folks at her office were offended when people even mentioned Jesus. "Do you go to church?"

"No, I don't."

"Do you consider yourself to be a Christian?" He hesitated. "Not really."

She focused on the barn. She needed to be sure she said what was on her mind. She took a deep breath and her stomach soured. There were so many thinks about Frank that she admired – he loved his niece and nephew, acting as a substitute dad since their parents' divorce. When he first met Cam, he seemed to pick up on the fact that he was a loner and probably would enjoy some company. He seemed intuitive, picking up on people's moods and doing what he could to make them feel better.

He'd been concerned about her all day. He was nice, caring, and kind. But, all of those things made no difference in their actually dating if he wasn't a Christian. *Lord, am I being too judgmental about Frank? I like him, and I want to spend more time with him.*

So disappointing. She'd only dated a few men in her twenty eight years – usually people she'd met at church. Even though the men she'd dated were Christians, not all of them were as kind-hearted as Frank. This was a lot for her to think about. What an exhausting, emotional day it'd been. Her attraction to Frank was deep, deeper than she imagined possible given the circumstances. She loved spending time with him and wished something could develop between them. However, she knew even if this was what she wanted, she had to follow the Lord's Word and not get involved with a non-Christian. She clenched her hands together, took a deep breath. "I don't think it's a good idea for us to spend time together socially anymore."

"Why?" He threw his hands up in the air. "We got along today. I like you, Emily. I want to get to know you better."

Wow, he actually admitted that he liked her. Well, she needed to be honest. "I like you too. I like so many things about you." She took a deep breath. "But, if I'm going to spend time with somebody, I want to make sure he's a Christian. My belief in God is the one thing that's constant and keeps me centered in this crazy world."

"We can still date and get to know each other better. You can't deny that we're attracted to each other."

Their attraction was so strong that it was a bit scary. Emily didn't know what she'd do with herself if she continued to see Frank and then fall for him. "Have you thought about getting help for your problem?" She would've asked him to give Jesus a chance, but, sensed that he wouldn't be open to talking about faith right now. Maybe once he'd battled his alcohol problem – or what she thought was an alcohol problem – he'd be more open to talking about accepting Christ.

"What problem?"

"Your drinking problem. There's an alcoholic support group at my church—"

"I'm not an alcoholic."

"You don't get drunk?" He narrowed his eyes, gave her a sideways look, but didn't say a word. "Your eyes were red this morning, and you said you didn't feel well. Were you sick, or were you hungover?"

He mashed his lips together. Uh-oh, he looked downright angry. She could his denying he had a problem. He focused on the cornfield. She thought about something else. She really needed to ask him about this. "Do you ever drive after you drink?"

He shook his head. "No. I only drink after I get home for the night." He peered at her. "Are you seeing anybody right now?" No wonder he changed the subject. He obviously didn't want to talk about his drinking problem.

"No."

"When was the last time you were in a serious relationship?"

"Why are you asking me this?" She didn't feel like talking about this right now.

He shrugged. "I'm just curious. I like you, and I want to know more about you."

She sighed. She really did *not* want to talk about Jamal. But, maybe she should. She'd been goading Frank into talking about something that he wanted to ignore, she supposed it wouldn't be fair for he to do the same thing. If Frank wanted to know about Jamal then she'd tell him about it. "I was engaged once."

"You were engaged? What happened?"

"I met Jamal in grad school."

"You went to grad school?"

She nodded. "I have a master's degree in agriculture. The only reason I was able to attend college is because I got a farm-sponsored scholarship. Both Jamal and I graduated a little over a year ago from the University of Maryland."

"Well, what happened? Why aren't the two of you married?"

"I thought we both wanted the same things. I felt he made some wrong assumptions about me, and he just couldn't accept me for the way I was."

"What kind of assumptions did he make?"

Dating Jamal had been such a waste of time. "Well, for starters, he didn't know I wanted to continue farming."

"He didn't know that? How could you be engaged to somebody who doesn't know that you love farming? I've only known you for a week, and even I can see how much you love farming. What were you all going to do?"

She frowned. "What do you mean?"

"Well, did you expect him to move into the house with you and your parents?"

Well, it would've been a little bit strange for her and her new husband to live on the farm while Dad and Laura were still here. She'd always imagined herself living in a home alone with her spouse while they started a family. "No, nothing like that. Since I thought we were planning to stay in the Baltimore County area, I was going to continue working for my dad. I'd planned on commuting to the farm from our new home."

"I still don't understand what the problem was. Besides, you were getting your degree in agriculture. Isn't that a clue that you'd want to stay in the farming business?"

She grinned. "Well, sometimes Jamal was pretty clueless."

"What did he want you to do?"

"He found a good job with an engineering firm, but it was located in Texas, so we'd have to move. He said once we were married and settled into our new lives in Texas, he didn't want me to work."

"What?"

She nodded. "He wanted me to be a stay-at-home wife and have kids and be a family woman." She shrugged. "Again, I just assumed he knew what I wanted. I would love to have my own family, but I wanted to be a farmer, too.

Since he wanted me to give up my profession, he obviously didn't know me very well."

"Is that the only reason you broke up?"

"Isn't that enough?"

He shrugged. "I guess, but I was wondering if anything else happened between you two."

"Well, he said he was a Christian, and I thought he loved the Lord like I did."

He frowned. "What made you think that he didn't love God?"

She wanted to make sure she said this the proper way. "We were very attracted to each other. When our engagement was official, he started pressuring me to make love to him. I told him I wanted to wait until after we were married, but he wouldn't let it go. We argued about it constantly, and we also argued about my continuing to farm after the wedding."

"Now I understand why you got upset at The Cheesecake Factory when I asked if you were a—"

"You've apologized." She didn't want to have a conversation to focus on what had happened earlier. "About Jamal, It got to the point where I dreaded his phone calls and visits until I finally gave him his ring back. I started to feel like a prop."

"A prop?"

She nodded. "Yeah. I felt like an actress or something."

"I don't know what you mean." He spoke

slowly, as if he were using mental energy to decipher her words.

"Well, after I met him, we didn't date for very long before we were engaged. Everything was so rushed that I felt like we didn't get to know each other very much. I sensed he was desperate to get married and have a family, and I was there, dating him. We were attracted, so he asked me to marry him." She sighed. "I don't think we were really in love. I felt like an actress, playing the role of his fiancée, without his knowing me as a person."

A warm breeze blew, tickling her cheek. When Frank took her hand, the warmth enveloped her fingers. "If you felt that way, why did you get engaged?" "Initially I wasn't honest with myself. I made excuses for our arguments and his behavior. Soon I got tired of making excuses, and I was just honest with myself. I sensed the Lord was telling me that Jamal wasn't the right man to spend my life with."

She mentally sighed when Frank seemed to be content with her answer.

They silently rocked in the swing, holding hands, his leg jiggling.

Headlights of a car turning into her driveway shined on them, and Frank dropped her hand. Kelly and Christine soon strolled toward the porch.

Frank frowned, staring at the women. "Who are they?"

CHAPTER 5

EMILY TOUCHED FRANK'S arm. "That's Kelly and Christine, my friends."

Kelly clutched a white grocery bag, and Christine held a box of Cinnabon rolls. Kelly grinned. "Hi. Christine and I didn't realize you'd have company tonight."

Emily gestured toward Frank. "He's not company. This is Franklin Reese; he's our new accountant."

Kelly raised one perfectly arched eyebrow. Figures she wouldn't hide the fact that she was checking him out. Kelly gave Frank a long, appraising look. She stuck out her hand. "Nice to meet you. I'm Kelly, and this is Christine."

Once Kelly shook Frank's hand, Christine did the same. "Hi, ladies."

Emily gestured toward the house. "I guess I'll see you on Monday, Frank?"

He stood, causing the swing to rock. "Yes, I'll be here on Monday." He exited the porch and waved to the women before he got into his car and drove away.

Kelly placed her hands on her hips, and Christine stood behind her. "He stood me up. This is the last time I accept a date with that loser!"

Sounded like her evening wasn't going to be ending right now. Kelly obviously wanted to talk about her dating woes. She couldn't even remember the name of the guy she'd mentioned recently.

They stepped into the house and Emily turned on the kitchen light. Kelly's black hair was swept into an elegant bun, and she wore a new pantsuit. Expensive perfume wafted through the room as Kelly tossed her grocery sack on the scarred kitchen table and Christine placed the Cinnabon box beside it. Wow, looked like she'd put a lot of effort into preparing for her date. Kelly pulled out two small ice cream cartons. "I got ice cream for both of us."

Christine pointed to her treat. "And I brought cinnamon rolls for myself." She rolled her eyes at Kelly. "She had the nerve to interrupt my lazy Saturday night. I was going to spend this evening lounging around in my silk pajamas and reading a book and eating my cinnamon rolls with a cup of coffee." She pointed at Kelly. "Then she appeared on my doorstep, distraught that Martin had stood her up, and she insisted we come to visit you so both of us could cheer her up in person. She stopped for ice cream on the way."

Emily plopped into a chair, placing her head in her hand. "I'm not hungry now. I'm glad you brought me ice cream, but I can't eat another bite." She pointed to her take-out container. "Frank and I ate at The Cheesecake Factory."

Kelly popped the ice cream carton open and fished a spoon from a drawer. "The Cheesecake Factory?" She sat, giving Emily a hard look. "Since when do you go out to The Cheesecake Factory with your business associates?" She grabbed Emily's arm.

"You'll never believe what Frank told me tonight." She glanced at the clock. "I wanted to call Mom and talk to her about it, but I'm sure she's in bed now." She told them what Frank said about the files he'd found on her father's computer, implying he may have been planning to sell their farm shortly before his death.

"Whoa." Kelly touched her arm. "That's deep. Do you think your stepmom knew about this?"

Emily shrugged. "I don't know. I sense she might be trying to protect me from something. . . ." She thought about it for a few minutes. "It makes my head spin when I think about it too much. My father is the last person who would sell this place. He always said he would farm until he died."

Kelly clapped Emily's shoulder. "Why don't we help you?"

"What do you mean?"

"Let's go and look through the stuff in your father's office. Maybe we can find something that will explain why he contacted the realtor."

Well, it was worth a shot. After Kelly had Christine had devoured their ice cream and cinnamon rolls, they strolled to her dad's office. Yeah, it'd be weird having others going through his stuff, but, she had no choice. She should've thought about doing this as soon as Frank told her about the files he found on the computer.

"I'll see if there's anything else on Dad's laptop. Since dad was a packrat, he had a lot of stuff. I know he dumped a lot of his recent stuff in that gray box in the corner."

Christine opened the box. "I'm happy to help, but, I don't quite understand what we're looking for."

Emily made herself comfortable in the office chair. "Neither do I. We just need to look and if we find something that looks…well, looks important, or may explain why dad contacted the realtor then just say something." They worked together in silence for over an hour. Christine and Kelly slowly flipped through the papers in the box while Emily looked through files on her father's laptop. Her phone pinged.

A text from her cousin Monica.

Been praying for you. Visit soon. Take a long beach swim.

Always nice to hear from her favorite cousin.

Thanks. Will do that soon. Hugs to you, John and Scotty.

"Monica just texted me. Do you remember her?"

Christine nodded as she flipped a paper. "Yeah, she's the woman who just got married a year ago and lives on the Eastern shore. I remember she's older than we are. One summer when she was staying at your farm, she drove all three of us to Baltimore to go to the movies."

"Well, remember she was at the funeral with her new husband?"

Kelly nodded. "Yes, I remember."

"She wants me to come visit her."

Christine glanced up from the paper she was reading. "Well you should. Laura took a nice long break, so you deserve the same."

Maybe Christine had a point. She loved being here on the farm, but, perhaps a change in scenery would do her some good. Laura sounded happier since she'd gone to visit her daughter. She wasn't sure if Laura's happiness stemmed from the change in scenery, or, if she was just ecstatic about seeing her kid again. She didn't know if she'd be able to leave the farm to visit Monica. The twins may miss a milking and she couldn't take the chance of the milking not being done. Besides, it'd probably be best if she stayed around until Frank finished up his audit.

Frank. She really didn't know what to do about him. As they continued looking through her father's files, she briefly told Kelly and Christine about her dinner with Frank and about his drinking problem and his lack of salvation.

Christine glanced up from the paper she'd been reading. "Maybe you can invite him to church and try to convert him."

"Convert him?"

Kelly stood, stretched and yawned. She slid her shoes back onto her feet. "I agree with Christine. Invite him to church and share the gospel with him. Maybe he's bitter about something and mad at God."

She couldn't imagine Frank agreeing to come to church with her. He'd turn her down, she just knew it. But, he'd mentioned their attraction to one another. Would he come to church just to spend some time with her – and maybe come to Jesus? "Do you really think I should ask him to visit our church?"

Christine nodded. "Of course you should. What would God want you to do?"

God would want her to share her faith with him. Hadn't she already done that earlier? Well, she could try again. *Lord, help me with this. Please help me share Your message of salvation with Frank. Also, please help me to figure out what was going on with my dad before he died. Amen.*

Frank pulled into the parking lot of the liquor store. He sat in the car for a few minutes, digesting all that had happened that day. He'd struggled all day and all evening about asking Emily out on a date. He was attracted to her, and even though he was upset with her decision about not spending time with him, he couldn't really blame her for her choice. He respected that she stuck with her beliefs, and he felt he needed to make more of an effort to put her out of his mind. When they were sitting on her porch, he had suddenly realized this was the first day in a long time that he hadn't thought about Julie. It was that thought that had bolstered him to ask her on a date.

Her refusal of his invitation was probably for the best. They were definitely not suited for one another. He exited his car. His cell phone vibrated in his pocket as he entered the shop. He glanced at his phone as he strolled toward the shelf that displayed his favorite scotch.

Trish. Hopefully the kids were okay. He stopped in the middle of the aisle. "What do you want, Trish?"

She hiccupped, jagged sounds of crying…what happened? "Are the kids okay?" If something was wrong with the kids, he'd have to be on the first flight he could find back to Chicago. She sniffed. "Frank." Her rough, jagged edge to her voice. Something was wrong. He needed to be sure he calmed her down.

"What's wrong?" He softened his voice.

Hopefully she'd speak soon so that he could figure out how to help her.

"Frank, it's Mark."

Somebody bumped into him and he dropped his phone. He picked it back up and rushed outside. He didn't know what he'd do if something happened to his nephew. He squeezed his eyes shut and took several deep breaths. His heart pounded so he leaned against the building. He gripped the phone. "Is he hurt?"

She sniffed. "No, not hurt." Her voice wavered as she cried again. "Mark met some friends to go to the movies at the mall." She sneezed and sniffed and blew her nose. "After the movie they went to a store and they were caught shoplifting. The security guard called me, and I had to go get him." She cried. "Frank, I don't know what to do with my son. He's been so angry since his father left."

Whew, this was serious. He relaxed. At least Mark was safe and he wasn't hurt. Now he needed to figure out what had to be done. Sometimes a boy needed another man to talk to. Since Mark's dad wasn't around very much, he needed to do what he could to help. "Did you want me to talk to him?"

"No, he's in bed now." She hiccuped and sniffed again. "Could you visit soon and spend some time with Mark? His father was supposed to visit the last two weekends, but he didn't show up. Mark's gotten worse since his father stood him up." She choked on a sob. "I'll understand if you can't come."

"No, let me check my workload, and I'll see if I can come down sometime soon." He rang off with his sister as he shoved the phone into his pocket. He re-entered the liquor store and lifted the bottle of scotch from the shelf. What he needed right now as a good, stiff drink.

Frank was still thinking about Mark a few days later as he sat in Emily's dad's office, going over the accounting ledgers. He'd called the boy twice and had told him that he was ashamed of what he'd done. Both times, Mark had spoken to him for about a half hour, which was phenomenal since his mom said he seldom said a word.

The screen door banged shut when Emily entered the house. Minutes passed. She was probably changing out of her barn boots before she came inside. He glanced at the time on the laptop.

Nine o'clock. He yawned. His brain was tired. He wished he didn't have the long drive back to Baltimore. She peeked into the room. He looked up, adjusting his reading glasses. Tendrils of hair spilled from her ponytail, giving her an earthy, mussed appearance. "Hey, it's late."

He blinked, pulled his glasses off, and rubbed his eyes. "I know. Why are you just now coming in from the barn?"

Sighing, she sat in a chair. "One of the cows was sick. I was just making sure she was okay. I think I'll call the vet tomorrow." She glanced around the office. "Why are you still here?"

"I'm missing some of your father's files."

She frowned. "What are you missing?"

He explained which financial papers he was looking for. "I'm going to have trouble finishing my audit if I don't find those papers."

"Christine, Kelly and I were looking to see if he had any documents that would help explain why he contacted a realtor." She shrugged. "We only looked for about an hour. I've been looking on my own when I can." She took a deep breath. "I'm sure the papers you're looking for are around here someplace." She stood and pulled out a drawer in one of the filing cabinets. "Have you looked in here?"

He nodded. "There's a few filing cabinets in the other corner that are locked. I didn't know where the key was."

Emily lifted a bright yellow mug from the desk and dumped the contents. Frank helped her sift through the mess, and his fingers brushed against hers. She spotted the key. "Here it is."

She rushed to the cabinet, placing the key into the hole. A soft click sounded as she unlocked the drawer. She pulled, but it failed to open. "I think it's stuck."The muscles in her thin arms bulged as she struggled to open the drawer.

He rushed to her side. Together they opened the drawer, and folders tum- bled onto the floor. He whistled softly, gazing at the papers. "Your father sure does keep a lot of stuff around."

Nodding, she massaged her neck. She looked tired. He figured she'd be going to bed soon. "My dad was a packrat. He kept everything. I hardly spent any time in this office. I don't really know what's in here. That's why Christine, Kelly and I were looking through the files earlier." Pulling out one of the folders, she flipped it open, finding notes written in pencil. "This makes no sense to me. It's just a bunch of numbers."

He glanced at the notes and frowned. "Well, whatever this is, it's not what we're looking for." He glanced at the cabinet again. "But we might need to go through this whole cabinet to find the papers we need."

She pointed to the gray box in the corner. "We were also going through that box as well. Maybe we should do this another time. I don't feel like looking through this stuff right now. It's late."

He didn't want her to leave, not yet anyway. Selfishly, he wanted to enjoy her company for as long as possible. He pulled a family photograph off her father's desk. "Is this your stepmother and your sister?"

She nodded, glancing at the picture. Emily looked like she was about eighteen in the photo.

"Yes, I think I was telling you about my sister when we had dinner at the pizza place."

He sat, still studying the photo. "Why do you look upset in this picture?"

"Because my father had just gotten remarried, and I was not eager to have a new female in this house. That picture was taken right before my sister, Sarah, left home. That's why you see her smiling. She was getting ready to leave the farm, and she was relieved because she always hated it."

"Were you angry that your sister left?"

She shrugged, glancing around the cluttered office. "It worked out okay. I love it here, and I don't mind being the only sister left behind to take care of the family business."

"Do you talk to your sister often?"

"No."

"Do the two of you get along?"

"It depends. Sometimes we do. She only calls me when she wants to borrow money."

"Really?"

She nodded.

"Does she pay you back?"

"Sometimes. We were never close even though we lived in the same house. My daddy used to say we were like oil and water."

"What happened to your real mother?"

"She died of breast cancer when I was fifteen. Things were pretty rough out here on the farm when she passed."

"Things were rough because you were grieving?"

"Sort of. Remember, I told you Sarah hated farming?"

He nodded.

"When Mom died, she refused to do anything. She wouldn't help out with the chores. She'd yell at my dad; she called me names." She shook her head. "My dad had to ask our church if they knew about any type of counseling services he could use for Sarah."

Now that sounded awful. After Julie had been killed, it'd been rough on him. Still was. "I'm sorry. That sounds pretty bad." Sexy and sweet. She sported a cowboy hat and holey blue jeans. Her socks even had holes in them. *I want to hug her and kiss her until she forgets all of her problems.* He used to do that to Julie all the time. Whenever she was upset about something, they'd talk about it, because she'd insisted. Then he'd kiss her…those slow lazy kisses always relaxed his wife.

She blushed as soon as she caught him staring. It was time to keep the conversation going. No sense in daydreaming. "If you don't mind my asking, how did you deal with your mom's death? It's obvious your sister turned rebellious."

"I spent most of my time in the barn or in the field with the cows, alone." She folded her arms in front of her. "It was awful. It took me a long time to get over losing my mom."

"Sarah's reaction reminds me of what my sister is going through now."

"What do you mean?"

"Remember I told you about her husband leaving?"

"Yes."

He told her about Trish's recent phone call and Mark's rebellious behavior. "I have to find some time soon to go and see Mark. I miss him, and I want to do everything I can to make him feel better."

"I'm sorry your nephew is hurting so much."

"I'm sure my sister's life would have been a lot better if she'd never married that guy."

She rolled her eyes. "You can't be sure about that."

Of course he was sure about that. Besides, Emily didn't even know Trish or the rest of his family. He'd know since they were his family. "I never trusted him, and I tried to warn her, but she wouldn't listen. Every boy needs a good, stable father at home, and it makes me mad that Mark's dad doesn't care."

"You really feel strongly about this, don't you?"

"Yes, it makes me upset when so many young boys are out there and they don't have fathers to turn to. I used to mentor kids at a rec center in Chicago."

"You used to mentor youth?"

He nodded.

"Have you done this since you've been in Maryland?"

"No." He'd just not had the time or desire to start mentoring yet. No way was he sharing the reasons why he'd stopped mentoring one year ago. Emily frowned and scratched the back of her head. "What's the matter?"

"Nothing. I was just thinking about something."

He looked at the bulging pile of paper. He didn't want to talk about Chicago anymore. "We have tons of stuff to go through. I hope we can find everything I need."

"How is the audit coming along so far? I'm sure my father's financial records are in good order."

"I can't comment until I'm finished. Do you understand everything we've been going through together? Are you having any problems with the financial software I showed you how to use?"

"I think I understand, sort of." She gestured around the office. "I'm still not used to handling all this. It's a lot of information for me to remember."

"Either myself or somebody in the firm can always advise you about financial matters."

"People are always telling me and Laura that we should have gotten more involved in the finances of our farm, and I'm starting to see they were right." She smiled. "But I'm just concerned about figuring out how this farm is doing and making sure we can continue the routine you've taught me during the last few days for our bookkeeping."

"Well, I still have to start a few audits at some other farms, and I'm at a standstill with your audit." He opened his briefcase and removed a business card. He flipped it over, writing his information on the back. "I'm leaving my business card. My work number is on the front, and I'm writing my home number on the back. My e-mail address is listed there, too." He pressed the card into her hand. Her skin..soft as warm butter. He could sit and hold her hand for a good long while. He took his time pulling his hand away. Downright awful trying to ignore their attraction. His skin heated whenever she stood near him for too long.

He sat at the computer and opened a document. He jiggled his leg. Man, he needed a drink. A drink, some dinner and maybe a good night's sleep. "Even though we've been through the whole budgeting and bookkeeping process together, I've still typed up notes for you and your stepmom about the accounting process for your farm. I tried to make the file easy for you to use." He pressed a few keys on the keyboard. "Laura might need my detailed notes since she wasn't here when I was teaching you everything."

"So, you're all finished?" He wished he could keep coming here each day, but being around Emily was torturous, knowing how she felt about his personal life and beliefs.

He told her the truth. "No, not completely. I have some loose ends to tie up, but I can do those at the office. Remember those papers I was telling you about?"

"Yes?"

"Well, when you find those, I can complete the audit." He glanced at the papers piled on the floor. "I don't want to waste time searching for something since we charge by the hour." He pulled a notebook from his briefcase. "I'm going to write down what I'm looking for." He scribbled the information, sensing Emily watching him the entire time. When he was finished, he pointed to the last two items. "I can't find your father's tax returns for the last couple of years."

Her mouth dropped open. "I know he filed his taxes—"

He touched her arm, and she calmed down. "I know he did. When I was going through his bank statements, I could see the direct deposits in his account from the IRS tax refund. But it'll still help me out if I could find those files." He glanced around the office again. "I know they're around here someplace."

"You want me to look for the things you have listed here?"

He nodded. "Please. When you find them, I can come back out here and complete my job, or, if you prefer that I not come, you can scan and e-mail the files to my office."

He wasn't sure what he should say or do. Saying goodbye and see you later didn't sound like a good idea. Suggesting that they meet for dinner at Leonardo's one night was a bad idea as well. She'd already made her stance clear about their dating, so, he wasn't sure what to do at this point. He'd caught her staring at him. She liked him…well…she appeared to like spending time with him. He liked her too, but now….well… what was he supposed to do? Since she'd had her conversation with him about his drinking and her religious beliefs, they'd continued working together in her father's office, sometimes making small talk. The attraction he felt for her refused to go away, so maybe it was best that he not return to her home after all.

"Frank, I can probably scan them and e-mail them to you if it's quicker. I don't want to waste your time by making you come out here." She tucked his card into her pocket and sat in the chair beside the filing cabinet, stacking the manila folders into a pile.

Frank stood beside the computer. His heart pounded like a kettledrum. "It's never a waste of time coming out here." The urge to kiss her rushed through him, but Julie's face hovered on the fringes of his mind. Emily dumped some folders into a box, mumbling about looking through them later. She picked up the container and walked into the kitchen, and Frank followed her, holding his briefcase and car keys. He wondered when he'd see her again. She placed the box on the table and walked him to the door. He stood on the porch and stared at her. Before he could stop himself, his lips brushed hers. She backed away, her pretty eyes widening.

"I didn't mean for that to happen." Crickets chirped, and the scent of animals and hay wafted around them. Her mesmerizing eyes were beautiful when she looked at him. He stepped back into the kitchen and closed the door, not wanting to leave anything unsaid between them.

"I'm sorry for kissing you. I hope you're not upset."

"Your lack of faith in God bothers me, Frank. Your drinking bothers me, too. But I enjoyed kissing you." She walked to the window, putting some distance between them.

"I know." She glanced at him. Her pretty eyes droopy with fatigue. "My drinking's been bothering me lately, too." Lately he'd been drinking more alcohol at night to get a buzz, and Trish was still calling him all the time, telling him he needed to get help.

She remained by the window, still looking at him. "Have you had a drink today?"

He shook his head. "No, not yet. That's why I'm still here. I didn't have a chance to tell you the other day that if I work late so my mind is tired, I may not drink as much when I go home." He clutched the handle of his briefcase. "But usually the memories and the nightmares bother me no matter what I do." The drinking always calmed him, soothed him, making it possible for him to fall asleep, even though there was sometimes a price to pay the following day. Since he'd started drinking more, he'd woken up sick to his stomach more often.

"You're haunted by something. What is it?" Her voice sweet as the chocolate she used in her candy, softened.

"Nothing I want to talk about right now."

"There's an alcoholic support group at my church—"

He held up his hand. "I don't want to go."

"But it might help you. You know, your lack of faith in God bothers me even more than your drinking." She turned toward the window again. "Maybe it's best that you've finished most of the audit for us."

The rusty hinges on the door squeaked as he opened it. "I'll e-mail you and your mother a report about what I've done so far. Just let me know when you've found those documents."

The screen door banged shut when he left. Emily remained at the window while he drove out of her driveway.

CHAPTER 6

THE NEXT DAY Emily awakened earlier than usual. She spent a leisurely hour reading a few psalms, finding comfort in the lyrical words. Both Jeremy and Darren arrived to help with the milking. After lunch the boys' father arrived plus a few other people she'd hired to help with the three-day chore of making hay. The day bustled with activity, and Emily was glad for the extra physical exercise. She hoped that if she was tired enough by the end of the day, Frank wouldn't dominate her thoughts.

During the day Emily daydreamed about his kiss. She again wished he'd listen to her and take her advice about accepting Christ in addition to getting help for his drinking. She also found thought about the role he was playing in his sister's life with her kids and about the fact that he used to mentor youth while living in Chicago. If Frank had children someday, he'd surely make a great dad.

She stretched and yawned after Jeremy and

Darren had helped her with the evening milking. She enjoyed a sub for supper then took a quick shower and changed before trudging to her truck. The repairman at the shop had stressed that she might want to start looking for a new vehicle. "This one is on its last leg and I don't know how much longer we're going to be able to repair it," he'd said.

She sipped from the thermos of coffee, thinking about the repairman's advice. She knew she would probably have to look for a used truck. She'd already called Laura, telling her what the repair shop had said about the truck and about what Frank had told her the previous day.

"Frank already called and told me everything," her stepmother had said.

"He did?" Emily didn't know why she was so surprised. Frank had mentioned that he needed to talk to her mother since Laura was the one who had requested the services of their firm.

"I can tell that something is heavy on your mind," her mother had said. "Did the accountant explain everything to you?"

"Yes, he explained everything in detail. Mom, when are you coming home? I miss you."

"I miss you, too. I promise I'll be home soon."

She continued to drive, putting the whole conversation out of her mind. She pulled into the parking lot of Dairy Christian Church for her volunteer committee meeting. During the meeting, she could barely keep her eyes open.

Christine and Kelly were present, and when it was over, the three friends exited the building together. "Girl, you sure do look tired." Kelly shook Emily's shoulder. "You're going to run yourself ragged working on that farm."

Emily stifled a yawn. "Today the workers and I cut the alfalfa with the haybine. Once it dries out over the next day or so, we're going to have to bale it."

Kelly grunted. "Sounds like a lot of work."

Emily nodded. "It is. I'm so tired."

Christine touched Emily's arm. "During the committee meeting, you looked like you had something on your mind."

"I do."

"What's the matter? Has Laura said something to upset you?" Kelly eyed Emily as they walked into the parking lot.

"No, I miss Laura, but that's not why I'm upset."

"Well, what's wrong?" Christine demanded. Their cars were parked side by side, and they stood in front of their vehicles. Emily debated about telling them what happened the previous evening.

"Why don't we go and get a snack at Leonardo's?" suggested Kelly.

Emily rubbed her tired eyes. "I'll go, but can't stay for long."

They sat at one of the two empty tables at the pizza joint. Leonardo's made the best creamy vanilla bean cheesecake. They purchased thick slices of cheesecake and iced tea. Emily sipped her drink before telling her news. "Frank kissed me last night."

Kelly's mouth dropped open. "Whoa. You're kidding!"

Christine raised her eyebrows. "Are you serious?"

Emily nodded. "I wasn't expecting it."

Kelly sipped her tea. "Are you going to see him again?"

Emily shook her head. "No, not unless I have to talk to him about the audit. I don't think it's a good idea for me to see him again. Once I find the documents he's looking for, I'll scan them and e-mail them to him. Once he's finished, I won't have to see him again." Man, that was hard. She *wanted* to see him again, and that was the problem. What was she going to do about it?

Christine leaned toward her. "You want to see him again. I can tell. How long do you think it will take you to forget about him?"

"I'm not sure. This is awful, but I miss him already. I know there's no hope for us."

Kelly sliced into her cheesecake. "There still might be hope for you and Frank. Leave everything in the Lord's hands and see what happens."

"Thanks, Kelly." She glanced at her other friend. "Christine, I notice you're wearing a nice pair of diamond earrings. Were they a gift?"

Kelly sipped her drink. "What do you think,

Em? Do you really think it was a gift? You know she probably charged her earrings."

Christine touched her earlobes, frowning. "I got these on sale at a new jewelry store that opened at Harborplace. I couldn't resist since they were a good price."

"Has anything else been going on with you, Christine?" asked Emily.

Christine placed her chin in her hand, gazing at her friends. "I do have a confession to make."

"What's that?" asked Kelly.

"I purchased these earrings for a reason."

"And what reason might that be?" asked Kelly.

"They had a meeting at work today. Some of us are going to be laid off within the next few months."

"Christine, I'm sorry." Emily touched her hand. "I know how much you like working there."

"So, you purchased the earrings because you were upset about the imminent layoff?" Kelly frowned. "I don't understand."

Emily peered at Kelly. Kelly had a habit of getting upset whenever Christine went on a shopping binge. "I think she's trying to tell us that she purchased the earrings because they made her feel better."

"Whatever." Kelly rolled her eyes. "You shouldn't be using material things to make yourself feel better, Christine. You said you might be out of a job soon, so buying a pair of diamond earrings won't make things better."

Christine shrugged. "I know they won't make things better, but they make me feel better. Do you understand?"

Kelly shrugged. "I guess."

Emily spoke to Kelly. "You're awfully quiet about what's been happening in your life lately. Have you heard from Martin?"

"Yes," Kelly responded.

Emily and Christine looked at Kelly expectantly. "Well?" asked Emily. "What did he say?"

"He said he forgot about our date the other night."

Christine asked, "Well, did he at least offer to take you out again?" "No," Kelly responded.

"How come?" asked Emily.

Kelly's mouth was set in a grim line. "You guys, no offense, but this is not something I'm ready to talk about right now."

Emily hugged her friend. "We don't mean to pry. If something's bothering you, then you know you can talk to me and Christine about it." Christine nodded, her dark eyes full of sympathy.

When they were finished with their snacks, Emily hugged her friends before she drove home. Once she'd read her Bible, she crawled into bed and said a brief prayer before she fell asleep.

CHAPTER 7

THE DAYS PASSED, and Emily still couldn't put Frank out of her mind. She thought about him daily, even though he no longer came to her house.

Memories of his kiss lingered, and she prayed, waiting for the feelings to disappear.

During the July Fourth holiday, she rode to Baltimore's Inner Harbor with Christine and Kelly to see the fireworks. Bursts of color exploded in the dark sky, illuminating the pedestrians and couples strolling the sidewalks. Longing pierced her when she observed couple after couple holding hands or nestling in each other's arms to watch the fireworks.

A few days following the July Fourth fireworks, Emily was thinking about the last time she'd seen Frank when she pulled into a parking space on Pratt Street, across from the Inner Harbor. She opened her purse, searching for coins to feed the meter. After the annual evening meeting with the Maryland farmers' association, she felt like taking some time and walking along the Inner Harbor alone. It was a blessing that both Jeremy and Darren came to milk the cows earlier, giving her the freedom to attend the event. She checked her watch. Eight o'clock. She still had some time to stroll around before the shops closed.

She continued searching for change, thinking about Laura. She missed her like crazy, and the loneliness on the farm was eating away at her. When she'd spoken to her a few days ago, she'd told her about the papers missing from her father's office and that she was searching for the paperwork Frank needed to continue his audit. She'd already found and e-mailed him a few of the files, but the rest of the documents were still missing. When she'd asked Laura about her father selling the farm, she'd claimed it was hard to know for sure what her father had planned on doing.

She gasped when Frank exited the upscale liquor store located on the water- front of the Inner Harbor. He clutched a large paper sack, and Emily was again reminded about how different their beliefs were and how their attraction seemed to escalate, in spite of their unshared faith. His head was down as he hurried toward his car. She couldn't resist. She just *had* to talk to him. She rolled down her window and yelled. "Frank!" He stopped and looked toward her with his piercing dark eyes. Her stomach flipped with pleasure. He clutched his paper bag and strolled toward her truck.

"Emily, what are you doing here?"

She inhaled the familiar scent of his cologne. She took another deep breath. Good gracious it was so good to see him. "I was at a local farmer's association meeting downtown. I just came over here to take a walk."

He remained silent as she glanced at the bag. He wiped the sweat off his brow. "I had to pick something up before going back to my apartment."

"Oh." Now what was she supposed to say? She couldn't invite herself up to his apartment. Maybe they could visit at the Starbucks down the street.

Frank relaxed against her truck. "It's hot out here. Did you want to come up to my apartment and cool off for a bit? I only live a few blocks away. We could share a few drinks."

She eyed the paper bag. "I don't think so." He should know that she wasn't much of a drinker.

"Emily, I was going to give you some lemonade. I made it myself. You don't have to stay long. I have some things concerning the audit that I was going to talk to you about."

She swallowed. Her throat was parched and a cold glass of lemonade did sound good. She started the ignition. "I'll follow you."

Once he'd gotten in his car, she followed him to his apartment building. A basketball court was outside, and a group of young people played a game in the intense summer heat. A few of the boys spotted Frank, calling out his name. "Hey, Mr. Frank, you want to shoot some hoops with us?"

He waved. "Maybe tomorrow."

Frank didn't say anything as the elevator drifted up to his floor. "You play basketball with them often?"

"No, not too often." They soon entered his cool loft apartment. "Sorry it's such a mess." He picked up a few clothes and threw them into the corner. Take- out Chinese and pizza boxes littered the area. Looked like Frank hated cooking. She supposed he could be too busy to cook since he worked late hours. She could certainly understand, because she'd been living off sandwiches and fast food ever since Laura left for Florida. The one thing she enjoyed making was her candy.

She felt the place could be charming and cozy with a woman's touch and a few decorations. The kitchen was spotless. Well, that was no surprise. He probably hardly ever used the kitchen. "How is your nephew doing?"

He lifted a pair of shoes and placed them in the hall closet. "He's doing a little bit better. He recently had a birthday, and I was able to go to Chicago for the weekend for his party."

She smiled, enjoying the grin that split Frank's handsome face as he spoke of his nephew. "I'm sure he was glad to see you."

"He was. We talked a lot, and I tried to get him to tell me what's been going on. I let him know I wasn't pleased with his shoplifting, and I hope my talking to him will influence him not to do it again."

"Did his father show up for his birthday?"

Frank frowned, tossing dirty socks into his room. "No, he didn't show up. He didn't even call." He shook his head. "He's such a lousy dad. I don't know what Trish was thinking when she married that loser."

She fingered the empty scotch bottle sitting on the coffee table. "Did you go to the liquor store to buy scotch?" Her voice wavered as she continued to look around the room. Empty beer bottles and a half-empty bottle of wine sat on the end table.

He took the bottle away from her and dropped it into the trash. "I told you things have been hectic in my life lately." A hard edge crept into his voice as he gathered items and placed them in the garbage can.

Clothes were strewn all over the place, and the hamper overflowed with garments. She wondered when he had last done his laundry. After he placed the paper bag in a kitchen cupboard, he pulled two cups from the cabinet and put several ice cubes into each. The ice popped when he poured the lemonade. Emily sat on the couch, and he handed her the cup. She took a drink, closing her eyes, relishing the sweet, tangy taste of the lemonade and the clean citrus scent of Frank's cologne. "You made this?"

He chuckled. "Yes, I made it."

She raised her eyebrows, enjoying another sip. "It's good."

"Thanks. All it is, is fresh lemons, sugar, and water." He shrugged. "It's no big deal." Both of them remained silent as Emily drained her glass. "Would you like more lemonade?"

"Please."

He returned to the kitchen with her empty glass so he could refill it. As he performed the chore, she was about to ask him about the audit when she noticed the wedding picture sitting on the coffee table.

She lifted the photo and saw Frank wearing a gray tuxedo, and his arm was around a bride. The woman's skin was the color of ripe blackberries. Her dark hair shimmered over her shoulders. Her arm was casually draped around Frank's waist, and her laughter seemed to jump right out of the picture.

She clutched the picture as he returned with the lemonade. "You're married?"

He shook his head. "I guess I should have mentioned it sooner. She's dead." He placed the picture on the coffee table face down.

She stared at the down-turned picture frame. "Dead?"

"My wife is dead. She was killed about a year ago."

"A year ago? That's so recent."

"I know. I still think about her a lot."

So many questions filled her mind that she didn't know which to ask first. "She's very pretty."

"Yes, Julie was beautiful."

Silence, thick and heavy, filled the room. She wondered what had happened to Frank's wife. "How long were you two married?"

"Two years."

"I'm sorry."

He stood and walked to the window, parting the curtains. Light streamed into the room from the streetlamps. "You know, I'm so sick of hearing that."

She joined him at the window. "Hearing what?" Tears glistened in his eyes. He quickly turned away. "What's wrong?"

When he didn't respond, Emily was tempted to let the subject drop. He wiped his eyes and dropped the curtain, returning to the couch. Emily joined him, still wondering about the death of his wife. "I miss my wife so much. It's one of the reasons I've started drinking again."

"I think your pain will lessen with time."

"I killed her, Emily. I killed my wife."

Mercy, he couldn't mean what he was saying. Could he? "I know you couldn't have killed her."

"It's my fault she's dead."

She touched his shoulder. "What happened?"

"Julie was raised in foster care."

She recalled the sad stories she'd heard about children in foster care. "That sounds rough."

"Yeah, but since she had been through so much with her brother during the time they were in foster care, they were closer than they should have been."

"What do you mean?"

"Her brother was into drugs. At one point, he owed somebody over a thousand dollars."

"Did she loan him the money?"

Frank chuckled, the sarcastic sound echoing in the room. "It could hardly be called a loan, because I knew he would never pay us back. I didn't understand why she kept bailing him out."

"So, did she give him the money?"

"I told her not to. She promised me she wouldn't meet him in that dangerous neighborhood where he lived to give him the money."

"But she went to meet with her brother anyway."

He nodded, tears falling down his cheeks. "Yeah, she went. Some stuff went down, and there was a bust when she was there. She was accidentally shot and died a few days later."

She hugged him. *Lord, please let me say the right words to comfort him.* "Did they catch the person who shot her?" She ended their hug and squeezed her hands together.

"Yeah, they caught him, and he's in prison. But I tell you what, if they hadn't caught him, I'd be going after him myself. I would have searched until I found her killer if the police hadn't gotten to him first."

"Why do you think this is your fault?"

"I should have realized what she was going to do. I should have gone with her. I knew how stubborn she was about helping her brother. Maybe I could have talked her out of it. If I'd reasoned with her, she may not have gone to meet with him and she'd still be alive."

"Or she could have thought about this with a level head."

He gave her a strange look. "What do you mean?"

"I know you miss your wife, and I can see how much you loved her, but it wasn't your job to ensure she always thought rationally. You're beating yourself up over something you had no control over. Julie knew what kind of crowd her brother hung out with, and I'm sure she knew about the danger of meeting him in that seedy area. Why couldn't she have figured out another way to get him the money? Could she have mailed him a check—"

"The type of people he dealt with wouldn't be waiting on a check."

She shrugged, still not deterred from making Frank see reason. "You mentioned to me that you were mad at your parents."

He nodded. "My anger at my parents started years ago when I'd started dating Julie. They didn't like the fact that she wasn't from a good family, and they didn't support my marriage."

"Is that the only reason you're angry with them?"

"Emily, when my parents rejected my wife, it was like they were rejecting me, too. I'll be honest with you and let you know that my parents did do something else besides reject Julie."

"What did they do?"

"When I got engaged to Julie, they did a background check on her and her brother. They didn't think she'd be a suitable addition to the family, so they told me the only way they would support my marriage would be if I made her sign a prenup."

Have mercy. The nerve. She just couldn't believe it. That was rotten. "I just want to make sure I understand what you're talking about. You're referring to a prenuptial agreement?"

He nodded. "Yes. They felt like she was just a gold digger, wanting to get into the family to get some of their fortune."

"You didn't ask her to sign it, did you?"

He shook his head. "No, I loved her, and I couldn't hurt her like that. When we got married, she wondered about the distant relationship we had with my parents. She was smart enough to know that my parents' cold reception of her was tied to her background, but she never knew about the prenup."

"So, they didn't talk to Julie much at all?"

He shook his head. "Not really. It was awful. When they distanced themselves from my wife, my relationship with them changed. When Julie died, they offered no sympathy. I feel like they thought she deserved what happened to her."

"Are you sure they feel like that?" She wouldn't be surprised if his parents felt awful about all that had happened. They might be sorry and Frank may have been too stubborn and too prideful to accept their apology.

He shook his head. "They never said it, but they just acted like they didn't care when she died. They didn't call or anything."

"Maybe they thought you didn't want them to call. Maybe they didn't want to make you angrier."

"You sound like you're defending them."

She touched his arm. "I'm just trying to make you see this rationally. What does Trish say about all this?"

"She says my parents want to start speaking to me again."

She said the first thing that came to her mind. "You'll need to forgive your parents for the way they mistreated your wife. I've told you this before, but the only one who can help you is God."

He gave her an icy stare. "What?"

"What about your faith in God? Haven't you prayed about your pain, asked God to help you forgive Julie's killer and to forgive your parents?"

She gestured around the cluttered room. "You can't drown your sorrows with booze."

"I don't care about God, and God doesn't care about me."

"How can you say that when you're not giving Him a chance?"

He huffed, running his fingers over his head. "Julie was saved not long after we were married. She tried to get me to accept Christ."

"What happened?"

His voice thickened. "Julie got killed." His dark eyes stared into hers. "I can't forget about that and accept God."

She prayed that God would lead her to say the right words. "Julie was saved? She's with Jesus now. Remember that."

He clasped his hands together. "Don't be preaching to me." He gave her a scathing look. "Besides, you have no idea what I've been through this past year."

She stood and stepped back, startled by his sudden outburst. She swallowed, her anger brewing like a slow stew simmering to boil. "I just lost my father, and I lost my mother years ago." She clenched her hands together. "I know what it's like to lose someone you love." She calmed down before she squeezed his hand. "Give God a chance. I still have the church program from last week's service in my purse." She opened her purse and pulled out the program and a pen. She circled one of the contact numbers on the back.

"The information about the alcoholic support group at my church is on the back." She pressed the paper into his palm. "The worship services are also listed. Devon Crandall is the leader for the alcoholic support group. They have weekly meetings, and I've heard good things about his work with the ministry."

He placed the program on the coffee table. "I'll think about it."

"I'll be praying for you." She hugged him before she left.

CHAPTER 8

THE FOLLOWING SUNDAY, Frank struggled to open his eyes before sitting up in bed. He cradled his aching head. "Oh man." The empty liquor bottle stared back at him, mocking his mistake. His sour stomach churned, and before long he ran to the bathroom and vomited. He relaxed against the cool, white-tiled wall, willing his rapidly beating heart to slow down. "God, I can't go on like this. I just can't." The nightmare about Julie haunted him again the previous night. He squeezed his eyes shut. Hopefully the unpleasant dream would vanish from his mind.

His cell phone chirped. He stood on wobbly legs and plodded into the bedroom. He lifted the phone from the table. Not bothering to check the caller ID, he answered the call. "Hello."

"Hi, little brother."

"Trish." The last thing he needed was a lecture from his sister.

"My goodness, don't sound so happy to hear from me." Sarcasm dripped from her voice.

Frank plopped back onto the bed. "I'm not feeling great right now."

"You're probably hungover."

He winced, ashamed of his nightly routine. "Are Mark and Regina okay?"

"The kids are fine. I didn't call to talk about them or about your drinking problem. I wanted to talk about Dad."

"What about him?" He cradled the phone between his ear and shoulder, grabbing the large bottle of acetaminophen on his bedside table. Popping the jar open, he shook four tablets into his palm and dropped them into his mouth. He drank from a bottle of water, swallowing the pills.

"He's still sick."

"Has he been to the doctor yet?"

She scoffed. "You know he hasn't. But he was telling me the other day that he wished you would talk to them again."

He shook his head, but the movement caused bullets of pain to shoot behind his eyes. Taking a deep breath, he laid back on the pillows. "I don't have time to listen to this."

"Well, you better make time. I think if you'd talk to Dad again, he might feel better. Maybe he'll be so glad to hear from you that he'll do whatever you ask him to, even if that's going to the doctor."

Still holding the phone, he entered the kitchen, willing his aching head to stop pounding. He opened the cupboard. The canister of coffee beckoned him. He removed the can and opened it, spilling coffee grounds into the white filter. "Trish, I have to go now."

"But, Frank—"

"I'll talk to you later." He ended the call and threw the phone onto the kitchen table. Soon drops of coffee splattered into the coffeemaker, filling the kitchen with an aromatic scent. He pulled a mug from the cupboard and filled it with the steaming brew, along with a generous portion of cream and sugar.

He entered his living room and sat on the couch and eyed his wedding picture. Guilty. Awful. That's how he felt right now and there wasn't a thing he could do about it. He blinked away unshed tears. He turned away from the wedding photo, continuing to sip his coffee. As the caffeine soothed his nerves, he set his mug down and returned to his bedroom. He found a box of his belongings, which he had never unpacked, sitting on the bottom of the closet. He dumped the contents, riffling through trinkets, old magazines, and books. Finally, he spotted his large black Bible, a gift from his deceased wife, among the clutter. Once he'd returned to the living room, he retrieved his mug, still holding his Bible. The old church program Emily had given him that week still sat on the coffee table.

He studied the piece of paper. Hopefully, he was making the right decision.

An hour later, Frank sat in a pew at Dairy Christian Church. Once the sermon finished, Frank mulled over the pastor's words about forgiveness. Heat, thick as the tropics, blasted at him once he stepped outside. People scurried to their cars, anxious to avoid the dreaded high temperatures.

He glanced around the sea of brown faces and stopped when he spotted Emily. Her white dress cascaded over her slim brown body, and her dark tresses were pulled into a severe ponytail, accenting her high cheekbones and full lips.

Kelly and Christine stood beside Emily. Laughter floated from the three women, and he wondered what they were talking about. Emily lifted her head, looking directly at him. Her smile faltered.

"Hi, Emily." He focused on Kelly and Christine. "Nice seeing you again, Kelly, Christine."

"Hey." Both Kelly and Christine greeted him at the same time. Kelly grinned. Her eyes sparkled as if she were hiding a secret. She whispered something to Emily before she rushed to her car.

He folded his arms in front of his chest. "I hope she didn't leave because of me."

"No, she's meeting somebody."

Christine spoke up. "I need to go, too. There's

a sale going on at some of the stores at the Inner Harbor, and I was going to go and look around."

Emily touched Christine's shoulder. "Is everything okay? I don't want you going shopping, buying things you can't afford just to make yourself feel better."

Christine shook her head. "I didn't lose my job, but I just discovered they only went through the first round of layoffs. They're going to do more within the next couple of weeks." She shrugged. "Maybe I'll just look around the stores and not buy anything."

"Did you want to share lunch with me instead?" Emily made the generous offer.

Christine shook her head. "No thanks. See you later, Em. Bye Frank." She then rushed to her car.

They stood awkwardly on the hot sidewalk. "I was shocked to see you here today, Frank."

He didn't know what to say about that. He was shocked that he was here, too. People walked around them, and she touched his arm, leaning in a bit closer. "You don't look like you feel very well, and your eyes are red. Are you sick?" He sighed. How was he going to answer her? "Did you have too much to drink last night?"

He pulled his arm away. "I don't want to talk about that right now."

"Is there something else you wanted to talk to me about?"

He touched her arm. "I never got a chance to

talk to you about the audit the other day when you came to my apartment."

"Oh, I'd forgotten all about that with everything you told me." She clutched the strap of her purse. "I'm getting ready to eat lunch. I could call you this afternoon if you want."

"Were you going out to eat?"

"Kelly, Christine, and I were planning to go to the Dairy Village Market for lunch, but they bailed on me. Christine is pressed to go to this sale, and I don't have the energy to go shopping with her. She shops for hours. So, we could go and get something to eat if you wanted."

They drove to the vegetarian restaurant. Emily ordered pancakes with fruit, a blueberry muffin, and a cup of tea. Frank's stomach was still sour, so he purchased a bottle of water. He took out his wallet to pay for their food, telling the cashier their order was together. Once they'd sat at their table, Emily poured maple syrup on her pancakes. "You didn't have to pay for my meal."

He waved her comment away. "This is a business meal anyway."

She bowed her head and blessed her food. Her long lashes fluttered when she opened her eyes.

"I'm surprised you're eating at a vegetarian place." Frank studied the crowded restaurant. Artsy folks with dreadlocked and cornrowed hair sat in groups. In the corner an elderly man sketched in a notebook. The cadence of African drums rolled from the speakers. The place had a good vibe. If he'd been in a better mood, he may have enjoyed himself more.

"It's just a change of pace. I've eaten at just about every place in Dairy since Laura's been gone. They don't have many places to eat here, and you know that I'm tired of making sandwiches every day."

"Speaking of your stepmother, do you know when she's getting back?" Laura had been gone a good long while. He wondered if she'd ever return.

Emily raised her eyebrows, her dark eyes full of suspicion. "Why do you ask?"

"I needed to talk to her about something important. I can call her, but I'd rather talk to her in person."

"What's wrong? Is the audit not going well?"

"It's not going well at all."

"What's happened?"

He thought about the latest development. "The numbers don't add up."

She frowned, staring into his eyes. "What do you mean?"

"There's something wrong. There are large amounts of cash that are unaccounted for."

She put her fork aside. "So, there's money missing?"

He ran his fingers over his head, frustrated. "Yes. When you e-mailed me those missing documents, I was able to piece this information together. I'm still trying to figure out what your father's done.

I was wondering if your stepmother might know something."

Emily pushed her plate away. "I doubt it. I already told you we didn't know much about the finances of our farm." She appeared pensive as she continued to speak. "Laura and I are lousy with numbers."

He frowned. "Really?"

"Yes. Back in grade school and even in college I struggled with math courses. The only reason I was able to graduate with my bachelor's and master's was because I hired a private tutor to help me with all my math classes. I can barely balance a checkbook."

"You're kidding."

She shook her head. "No, I'm not kidding. I've struggled with math my entire life, and Laura told me she's never been good with math either. My dad had this natural mathematical ability, so we just let him handle all the money. You probably wouldn't understand since you crunch numbers all day. Before you showed up, I tried to teach myself accounting. It was a disaster. I didn't understand anything."

His mathematical abilities had always come naturally, so it was hard to understand how someone couldn't balance a checkbook. He touched her hand. "Don't worry about it. I'm sure there's some explanation. Did you find your father's missing tax returns?"

"No, not yet. I've been looking during my spare

time. We've been baling hay recently and the hot temperatures have been affecting our corn crop. I've been busy on the farm a lot, and I've also been thankful that one or both of the brothers have been showing up for both the evening and morning milkings."

They sat in silence for a few minutes before Emily began eating her pancakes again and Frank drank his water. Emily leaned toward him. "Have you been okay? You have circles under your eyes."

He set his water bottle back on the table. "Remember you told me about Devon Crandall?"

"Yes, I remember."

"I showed up to a meeting."

She grabbed his hand. "Are you serious?"

"Yes. But I couldn't go in."

She squeezed his hand. "Why not?"

"I just couldn't. I stood outside the door for a minute. I don't think anybody saw me." He gazed out the window at a couple who walked by holding hands. "Maybe I can give up the alcohol on my own."

"You told me that you'd had alcohol problems before when you were in college. How were you able to quit back then?"

He recalled that time in his life. "They had AA meetings near campus. But. . ."

She squeezed his hand again. "But what?"

"To tell you the truth, I've been doing some heavy drinking for over a year now. Back when I was in college, I'd only been drinking for a few months before it started becoming a problem. I think it might be harder for me to quit this time."

"Maybe you should give it another try. Maybe you could have somebody go to the meeting with you."

"Going to that group of people makes me nervous."

"Why?"

"I don't know."

"Devon is an understanding man. Maybe you can just meet with him to talk about what you've been going through."

As she ate her lunch, Frank gave Emily's advice serious thought.

CHAPTER 9

DURING THE FOLLOWING month Emily kept busy on her farm. How glorious when they had almost two straight days of rain. The claps of thunder and bursts of lightning thrilled her, making her giddy. The heat and dry weather had worried her, and the moisture was just what her crops needed to thrive.

She'd called Laura about Frank's questions, but her stepmother was shocked to hear about the missing money. As far as Laura knew, all of her father's financial information was in his office. Laura had mentioned it was certainly possible that there were files elsewhere in the house, so Emily said she'd keep looking around to see if she could find any missing documents that would help account for the missing funds.

One morning after the milking was done Emily and Jeremy stood at the sink, rinsing the equipment and cleaning the barn. The slender teen turned toward Emily. "My mom told me to ask if your mother was coming home soon."

"She said she was coming home shortly. I've been talking to her every day." She glanced at him, wondering if he understood the pain of losing somebody. It was possible that being around the farm made Laura sad since she missed her husband. "I don't want to keep bothering her about when she's coming home. But I do miss her a lot." She gave the teen a smile and continued rinsing her equipment. She was a little hurt that Laura had not called to wish her a happy birthday. "Make sure either you or your brother or both of you are here tonight to milk the cows."

"Oh, we'll both be here." He held up his phone. "You can even call us to make sure we're here if you want to."

A few hours later, Kelly and Christine arrived at Emily's farm, and the three women rode to the state fair together. When they arrived on the fairgrounds, they assisted the rest of Dairy Christian Church's hospitality committee. In addition to serving pound cake and bottled water, they'd planned on doing face painting to entice the children to their booth. After working all morning, Emily was ready for a break.

"Hi, Emily." Frank's voice greeted her ears like a soothing lullaby. Turning toward him, she enjoyed the sensations that skittered across her skin when he touched her arm.

"Frank. I didn't know you'd be here."

"The fair was advertised in the church bulletin,

and you told me you were on the committee." His dark eyes sparkled. "Can you take a break?"

She checked her watch. "Is it okay if I take my lunch break now?"

Kelly completed a child's face painting. "Why don't you go ahead with Frank and have a good time." She reached for her purse beneath the booth. "If you don't mind, you can bring me back something to eat." She told her what she wanted for lunch. The rest of the committee members also produced money for lunches since they weren't interested in walking around the fair.

Frank and Emily strolled away from the booth. "Why did you come to the fair?"

"I came to see you. Since I haven't been coming out to your farm lately, I've missed you."

His soothing word made her feel good all over – like relaxing in an intoxicating warm bubble bath. She needed to be truthful with him. "I've missed you, too."

They strolled around the grounds then bought hot dogs from a vendor and sat at one of the picnic tables. She bit into her hot dog and drank some soda. She touched his arm. "How have you been?"

"I've been okay." He stared at the crowd populating the fairgrounds. "Well, I wish I could be better."

She took a deep breath before asking her next question. "Have you been drinking?"

"I've been working late, and that helps a little bit, but it doesn't keep me away from the alcohol."

"Did you call Devon Crandall?"

"No."

"Why not? He's very easygoing, and I'm sure he wouldn't mind if you called him." He didn't say anything. "Are you coming to church again tomorrow?"

He smiled before sipping his soda. "Yes, I plan on going."

"You should try and talk to Devon after church tomorrow. He's one of the ushers. He's well over six feet tall with gray hair. His wife is so short that they look funny together because of his height."

"Okay, I'll keep that in mind."

She bit into her hot dog. "How are Mark and Regina doing? Does Mark still call you a lot?"

He grinned. "Thanks for asking. Both of them are doing fine. Mark has been calling me almost every day. If I don't hear from him, I'll call. I'm glad he hasn't gotten into any more trouble, and he seems excited to be back in school."

"I'm glad to hear they're doing well." She observed the colorful tents on the grounds for a few seconds. "Oh, Frank, I almost forgot to tell you." She abandoned her hot dog and clenched her hands together.

"What's wrong?"

"Nothing's wrong. This morning I found the tax returns you were looking for. There were also some other bank statements, too."

He frowned and finished his food. "Other bank statements? What kind of account is it? Is it checking, savings, money market?"

She shrugged. "I'm not sure."

"Were they to another account, a different one than the one I was looking at?"

"I think so. I didn't realize he had an account there. This bank is all the way on the other side of Baltimore County."

"Did you check the balance? Maybe that's where the missing funds are." She told him the sum that was in the account.

His eyes widened. "Whoa. Why would he separate that much money into another account? It must be either a money market, savings, or retirement account."

"You know, it's the strangest thing. . ." He sipped his soda. "What?"

"I didn't find them in his office."

Frank frowned again. "Where did you find them?"

"They were stuck in a manila folder in the hall closet." She shook her head. "I don't understand why he had all his other tax returns on his computer with the exception of those two. Why would he separate them like that?"

He wiped his mouth with a napkin. "I'm not sure. If you don't mind, I'd like for you to scan them and e-mail them to me as soon as possible. That way I can complete the work for your farm."

Questions popped through her brain. If Frank

finished his audit for their farm, did that mean she would have no contact with him anymore? He touched her hand. "What's the matter?"

She shook her head, not wanting to voice her concerns. "Nothing. I'm okay."

When they were finished with their lunch, they strolled the fairgrounds again. Frank walked back with her to the booth before he left the event. Christine and Kelly immediately surrounded her, wanting to know what was going on between her and Frank.

"What's wrong, Emily?" Christine asked the question as they pulled into Emily's driveway.

Emily shook her head. "Nothing's wrong. I'm just tired."

Gravel crunched beneath their feet as they walked to the front door. Emily yawned. It sure would be nice to lay down in her soft bed and get a good night's sleep. She stopped walking, looking at her friends. "Do you guys really feel like visiting right now? I was going to go to bed."

Christine patted her shoulder. "We'll try not to wear you out too much. Let's make some coffee and talk for a bit."

"Yes, a cup of coffee sounds like a good idea." Kelly agreed.

Emily trudged up the steps, concerned about the full darkness cloaking her house since she usually left the porch light on. She made a mental note to change the lightbulb. The hinges on the screen door creaked as she entered.

"Happy birthday!" The dark kitchen flooded with light, and a sea of familiar faces filled the room.

Emily placed her hand against her quivering mouth. Seeing all of her friends together…it took her a few seconds to say anything, she was so excited. "Oh, my goodness."

"Hey, Emily!" Laura Cooper strolled into the kitchen.

"Mom!" Emily shrieked, pulling the older woman into an embrace. The familiar scent of Laura's jasmine perfume filled Emily with euphoria, and tears gathered in her eyes.

Kelly pressed a tissue into Emily's hand. "Happy birthday, Emily!"

She glanced at Kelly and Christine. "You two kept this from me all day!" Emily released her mother, wiping her wet eyes. "Mom, you look thinner since you left."

Laura swatted Emily's arm. "I've been fine."

Emily shook her head, still trying to take in the whole atmosphere. "I was wondering why you didn't call me today!" She temporarily ignored the numerous guests, eager to speak with Laura.

"Honey, you know I wanted to call you today, but I can't keep secrets. I know I would've accidentally said something to spoil Kelly and Christine's surprise!"

Emily's joy bubbled to the surface. Crepe paper streamers fluttered when the wind blew in from the open screen door.

Emily stared at the crowd, touched. "This is one of the biggest surprises I've received in my entire life."

A strong, unique scent filled the air. Emily rushed over to the stove, opening the lid on one of the pots. "You made me chitterlings!" The pig intestines, cooked to perfection, were one of her favorite foods. Serving herself, she piled some on a plate and placed a generous amount of mustard on the side. She took a bite, savoring the flavor.

Her friends from church were present as well as Cameron. As she continued to eat her food, Christine took her aside. "I'm sorry about Cameron coming."

"Why is he here?" Emily popped a huge bite of chitterlings into her mouth. The greasy pork taste was delicious.

Christine rolled her eyes. "When we were at the grocery store getting the stuff for the party, Cameron was nearby and we didn't realize it. He overheard us talking about your party, and he asked if he could come. I couldn't tell him no." Later, when she opened the gifts, she was pleased to see the assortment of perfumes and lotions people gave her. She also received some gift cards to her favorite clothing store. However, she was shocked Cameron gave her pearl earrings. "Thanks, Cameron," she said, giving him a small smile.

The party lasted until well into the night. Once the guests were gone and Christine and Kelly had put away the leftovers, it was close to midnight, but Emily was still high on energy. She sat on the porch with her stepmother on the large swing. They swayed in the gentle summer breeze. It felt good, downright nice to have Laura home again. "How're your daughters doing?"

"Lisa's fine. We had a nice visit."

"Has Becky been calling you much?"

Laura looked away for a few seconds. "You know how strained things are between Becky and me. She calls every few weeks. I just wish we could settle our differences and have a better relationship. I've been praying for a better relationship with both daughters for a long time, so I'm hoping things can change between us."

Emily patted Laura's shoulder, praying things worked out with her girls. She knew Laura had divorced at a young age and her ex-husband had been granted custody of their two small children. Her husband had hired a good lawyer, and he'd used Laura's past convictions with drugs against her. She'd cleaned her life up by the time she was married and had children, but her husband's lawyer was able to convince the judge that the father would be a better parent because he'd never had the substance abuse problems Laura had had in the past. Laura had told her that she always regretted losing custody of her children, even though she had generous visitation rights. Her daughters were now in their early thirties, and she wondered if the strained relationship they had was due to the fact that Laura did not raise them herself.

Even though they'd talked about it on the phone, she told Laura about the audit and about finding her father's tax returns. "Mom, we really should have been more involved in the financial side of things."

Laura touched Emily's hand. "Honey, I know we should have. But there's nothing we can do but move forward."

Emily again mentioned the correspondence Frank had found with a Realtor in her father's files. "He said it appeared as if he was planning to sell the farm. I told him he must be mistaken. Are you sure Dad never mentioned this to you?"

Her stepmother remained silent as the swing continued to rock. "Mom, what are you hiding?"

"Honey, I wasn't completely honest with you when you mentioned this to me before. I didn't want to tell you this, but Frank is right. Shortly before your father died, he was contemplating selling this farm."

Emily's mouth dropped open. "But. . .why? Daddy always loved farming." This was awful, plus, her dad never said a word about it to her. The hurt pierced her like a fiery arrow of pain.

She took a deep breath and pressed her hands together.

"I know, but he confided to me that for the last two years profits had been bad for the farm."

Emily shook her head. "I don't believe it. Why didn't he ever say anything to me about this?"

She touched Emily's arm. "He didn't want you to worry about it, that's why."

"But I still don't understand. Frank would have said something about our farm not being profitable, wouldn't he?"

"Emily, remember he's not finished auditing the books." She frowned.

"What's wrong, Mom?"

"I didn't want to tell you this, but…before your father passed, I could see how much the financial strain of the farm was bothering him. I tried to get him to hire an accountant to go through his tax returns and stuff to see if he may have been missing some important write-offs."

"And he didn't agree to do it, right?"

"He reacted worse than you did when I made my suggestion. He got angry with me. You were at a church function that night, and we argued about it for hours. Honey, your father was good with numbers, but he was not an accountant and he was no CPA. I know we hear about farms selling out sometimes, but I knew there were farms that did pretty well. I figured if he got advice from an accountant, he may have gotten an even better return when he filed his taxes and when he invested his money. You always hear about tax laws changing and such, and I wanted him to see a professional about his farm."

Emily rubbed her head. "Is this why you wanted Frank to audit our books?"

Laura nodded. "Yes. I've been worried about this for a long time, and since your father is gone, I'm even more worried about it. We seem to be making it financially day by day, but I just want to make sure your father knew what he was doing when he accounted for this farm and when he filed his taxes in the past."

This newfound information made Emily's head ache. She silently prayed for strength before deciding to tell her mother something else that was on her mind. "Mom, I think I have a big problem."

"What is it? Has something else happened since I've been gone?"

"Well, you know I've been spending some time with Frank."

"You like him, don't you?"

"Yes, how did you know?"

"You say his name like you're familiar with him. I know he has feelings for you, too."

"How do you know that?"

"Just from talking to him on the phone. He seems concerned about the farm, more concerned than a stranger should be. When I speak to him, I feel like I'm talking to a friend." They were silent for a few minutes as they continued to rock on the swing. "Maybe the Lord is trying to tell you it's time to move on since your engagement to Jamal ended."

"I don't think so." They rocked well into the night, and she told her mother all about why Frank was the wrong man for her.

CHAPTER 10

"GOD WILL NEVER leave you nor forsake you. I want all of you to remember that when you leave church today." Pastor Brown completed his sermon to the congregation. Frank closed his Bible, still thinking about the words. He sat in the pew beside Emily and her mother. After all these weeks, he'd finally gotten to meet Laura.

When the service ended, Emily took Frank's hand, causing sparks of delight to dance through his fingers. She gestured toward Laura. "We're going out to lunch at Leonardo's. Did you want to come with us?" Frank shook his head. He glanced at the ushers still in the back of the church. "In case you're interested, Devon Crandall is the one on the left."

He squeezed her hand. "Thanks." Emily and Laura exited the church, and Frank swallowed, still working up the courage to approach the older man. He breathed deeply as he walked up to the usher. "Devon Crandall?"

The man smiled at Frank, his dark eyes warm and friendly. "Yes?"

"My name is Franklin Reese."

The usher smiled, shaking Frank's hand. "I've noticed you coming to our church recently. It's hard not to notice a new member in a church this small."

Frank sighed, not wanting Devon to get the wrong idea. "Well, I'm not a member of this church."

"If you're a member of God's family, then that makes you a member of this church."

"No, I don't think I'm a member of God's family either."

The man's smile faded as he squeezed Frank's hand. "You look like you need somebody to talk to, son."

"I don't want to hold you up."

"There's no hold up." He placed his hands on his hips, continuing to assess Frank. "People are always telling me how perceptive I am, and right about now I think you need a friend. Would you like to come to my house for lunch?"

"I don't want to bother you."

"Oh, it's no bother. My wife usually cooks too much food anyway." He patted his gut. "I certainly don't need those extra calories."

"Okay." Devon seemed kind and perceptive. Truth be told, he did not a friend right now, really bad. Sometimes, he felt like he was losing his mind, trying to sort through all of his problems.

Sometimes, the problems seemed to rest on his shoulders heavily, like placing too much weight on a wooden beam – the beam could only hold so much weight – soon it would shatter and break. Sometimes, when he drank alcohol, the alcohol relieved some of the pressure that rested on his shoulders.

Devon beamed. "Good. I'll just let my wife know you're coming. You can follow us to our house."

A half hour later, Frank shared lunch with Devon and his wife. The tiny salt-and-pepper-haired woman welcomed Frank into her home, embracing him warmly. When he'd commuted to the Crandalls' house, his queasy stomach had settled from his drinking binge the night before, and he was able to enjoy the tasty pot roast, mashed potatoes, and green salad. "You and Devon can have your dessert in the library." Devon's wife made the suggestion with a smile. After placing coffee and cake on a silver tray and carrying it into the library, she left the room to give them some privacy.

The blinds were open, and bright sunlight spilled into the room. "So, tell me, Franklin—"

"You can call me Frank."

"Okay, Frank. Tell me why you approached me in church."

Frank stirred his coffee, wondering where to start. Did he explain the anger he had for his parents and the death of his wife, which drove him to drink? Did he tell of his budding feelings for Emily? "Since Paul Cooper died, Laura and Emily needed help with their bookkeeping. They contacted my employer, and I was sent to do the job. Emily mentioned you ran an alcoholic support group."

Devon nodded, serving the chocolate cake. "Yes, I do. I've been running it for over ten years. The group is not just for members of our church; it's also there for people in surrounding churches. We meet every week in the basement of the church."

"I know. I showed up once, but couldn't enter the room."

Devon didn't seem surprised about Frank's actions. "You made it to the meeting, so that's a big step. You should come in next time. We'd be glad to have you. So, tell me what's been making you drink."

"My parents never accepted my wife because of her background. My family's pretty wealthy, and my parents thought they knew who would be the best wife for me. They didn't support my marriage, and when my wife died, they never apologized for not accepting Julie into the family." He briefly told of how Julie was killed, and then he added, "I felt so bad, Devon. Not only did I lose my wife, but. . ." He looked away and didn't realize he'd been crying until Devon gave him a tissue. "I lost a child." He shook his head. "A few days before Julie died, she told me she was pregnant." He wiped his wet eyes and blew his nose. "I just wish there was some way I could've stopped her from going to meet her brother that day." He balled his hands into fists. "I feel so bad. The alcohol is the only thing that makes me feel better anymore." Devon squeezed Frank's shoulder.

Once Frank was calmer, Devon asked him a question. "When does the urge to drink happen?"

"Usually hit in the evening, after working a full day."

"Frank, I'll be praying for you every day, but you really need to meet with the alcoholic support group weekly." He gave Frank a business card. "You can call me anytime you want to, but I'm warning you, I'll be calling you every day, too." He stroked his chin. "By coming to me, I think you've admitted to yourself that you have a problem. Also, I want to point out that you can't handle this sort of problem alone. Not only do you need help from the support group, but you need to find help in Jesus. If you'll just accept Him as your Savior, then the load you carry on your shoulders will become lighter. Remember what the pastor said this morning: Jesus will never leave you nor forsake you."

Frank certainly felt left and forsaken, but he didn't know if he'd find the courage to surrender his life to Jesus.

CHAPTER 11

A FEW DAYS LATER Frank met with his boss and informed him of his final discovery for the Coopers' farm. "You'll need to meet with the wife since she's the one who initiated the audit," his boss had advised. He again wondered about the partnership that had been hinted when he'd first arrived in Maryland. He didn't want to say anything about it since he'd still not been doing the farm and ranch accounting for very long. He figured it'd be best to wait some more time to see what happened.

After speaking to his boss Frank rushed over to the Emily's. He sat in his car in front of the Coopers' farm. It was midafternoon, and he was scheduled to meet with Laura Cooper alone. When he'd called that morning to make the appointment, she'd said to come that afternoon since Emily would be at the grocery store. His thoughts wandered to the previous night. The urge to drink had slammed into him after Trish called, again saying that their father was not doing so well. He'd picked up the phone to call his dad but found the old anger festering in his heart like a canker sore. Instead of turning to drink, he'd called Devon Crandall, who'd again stressed that Frank needed to find relief in Jesus. Devon had encouraged him to come to the next support group meeting, and he'd also told him to discover more about God. "Read the New Testament, Frank. It'll tell you about Jesus' nature." He'd spoken to the man for more than an hour. After tossing and turning in bed for a long time, he'd finally gone to sleep—without taking a drink of alcohol.

He got out of the car and walked to the screen door. The urge to drink almost consumed him, but he forced himself to think of Emily, the Cooper farm, and the news he had to deliver. Taking a deep breath, he rapped on the door. Laura sat at the table, reading her Bible and drinking a cup of coffee. The woman looked up, smiling. "Frank." She placed a marker in her Bible and closed it. "Frank, come on in." When he sat at the table, she touched his hand. "You seem a bit agitated. Are you okay?"

"Not really."

"Is something wrong?"

"I'm fine. I wanted to talk to you about the audit. I don't think Emily looked through all the financial papers in that file she found."

"What are you talking about?"

"Your husband had Excel spreadsheets keeping

track of winnings and losses at a gambling casino over in Delaware. I've found evidence that he was spending large sums of the farm's profits at a casino. He kept records of what he had spent and how much he owed the farm from his gambling debts."

Laura cried softly. "I thought he had stopped gambling. He was going to a support group."

Her reaction caught him off guard. "You knew about this?"

"Yes, he did this a long time ago, but he promised me he'd stopped. I can now see it was all a lie." Frank found a box of tissues on the counter, and he gave them to her.

"Emily doesn't know?"

"No, neither of his daughters knew about their father's bad habit. I didn't think it was necessary to tell them since he'd told me he'd stopped."

If Emily and Laura wanted to start keeping track of the accounting records and tracking the profitability of the farm, then he didn't see how he could hide this information from Emily. He relayed his concerns to Laura.

"I understand. I just don't know how to break it to her. She thought her father was perfect." She blew her nose and looked at him as if to seek comfort. "I don't know how I'm going to tell Emily. But I don't have a choice." She sniffed. "Oh Lord, please help me."

"Mrs. Cooper, that's not all I needed to tell you. I believe your husband falsified his tax returns."

With shaky hands, she covered her mouth, continuing to cry. "Do you mean he owes money to the government?"

"Yes. He grossly understated his revenue, and I know he owes the IRS some money. . .a lot of money. He's falsified his tax returns for the last two years." He told her how he couldn't find the tax returns for the last two years and that Emily found them hidden in the closet. "Did you look at the tax returns before you signed them?"

"Paul took care of all the finances. When he told me to sign the tax returns, I just trusted the numbers were accurate." She wiped her tears away. "Will we have to lose the farm to pay the back taxes? This farm means so much to Emily. She would die if she lost this home."

"You could lose your farm. But you'll have to let her know what happened. Usually in situations like this, the IRS will want their money back. They might work with you and Emily to set up a payment plan." When she had pulled herself together, he finally spoke again. "When are you going to tell Emily?"

She wiped her nose. "I'll tell her before the end of the day. She deserves to know."

He tried to make her feel better. "Mrs. Cooper, I think your husband may have been keeping track of all this because he was planning on replacing the money he lost back into the farm."

She nodded. "He's done this before, a long time ago. He thought if he kept at it long enough, he would win the money back. But sometimes, when he did win back the money he'd lost, the temptation to gamble it away again was just too great." She shook her head. "I'll never understand why this happened, but I promise I'll talk to Emily about it today."

Later that day Emily returned from the barn and stifled a yawn. Man, she was tired. She needed a nap before doing the evening milking. She quickly changed and got into her soft bed. She covered up with her quilt and fell asleep. The jarring ring of the phone interrupted her sleep. She wasn't going to answer it. The bed felt so comfortable – like sleeping in the middle of a comforting cloud. Emily turned her head on the soft pillow, snuggling deeper into her blankets, hoping to get a few more minutes of sleep before milking time.

Laura's footsteps pounded on the floor, and Emily's door flew open when she entered. "Emily, you've got to wake up." She opened the blinds, and sunlight spilled into the room. Emily regretfully broke her midday nap. "Mom, what's wrong?"

Laura paced the room, her mouth set in a grim line. "Becky's had her baby! They just gave her a C-section at the hospital."

Emily was awake in minutes. This was serious. *Lord, please help Laura's daughter and her new baby. Please let them be okay. Please be with Laura and the rest of Laura's family, too.* She sat up in bed. "But Becky's only seven months pregnant. What happened?"

"They think the size of her fibroids caused her to go into early labor." Her stepmother shook her head. She sat on the bed and grabbed Emily's hand, closing her eyes. "Lord, please be with us during this trying time." Her voice filled the room as they lifted up the plight of Becky's baby. When their prayer was finished, she squeezed Emily's hand.

"They say the baby's chances of survival are good." Her mother shook her head. "I've got to get out there."

Emily's heart filled with dread at the thought of Laura leaving again, but she knew it was for the best. "I know you do, Mom."

"I hate leaving you so soon."

Emily shook her head, patting Laura's frail shoulder. "Don't feel bad about it. Becky's got two other children, and since it's the busy season at her husband's job, you know he's going to be working some serious overtime now." Both of Becky's children were under five, so her stepmother would have her hands full. "Don't overdo it, Mom. I don't want your back to go out on you again." The last time that had happened, she'd been in bed for a week, barely able to move without being in pain.

"Honey, I won't." She glanced at the clock. "Since Becky's had a C-section, I know it's going to be hard for her to get around for about a week or so. I want to try and get a flight out of here today."

One of Laura's friends from church soon arrived to take her to the airport. Emily was sorry to see her stepmother go so soon after returning from her trip to Florida, but she knew it was necessary for her to be there to assist her daughter with her children.

That evening Emily was out in the barn with Darren milking the cows when her cell phone chirped. She told Darren to continue milking alone for a few minutes and answered the call. "Hi, Laura."

"Emily, with all the excitement about Becky's baby, I forgot to tell you about Frank's audit."

Emily frowned. "What about it? Is Frank finished?"

"Emily, you need to call him now. I'm not very good at explaining financial things, and he can do a better job of it."

The phone crackled a bit. "Mom, I can't hear you very well."

"Honey, I think I'm losing the connection, but I want you to contact Frank!"

After ending the phone call with her mother,

she called Frank. "Hi, Emily." His deep voice sounded so good and soothing. Just hearing him speak made her feel better.

She told him about the birth of Becky's baby. "Mom's already left. She told me that I needed to call you about the audit."

"Can I come by tomorrow night?"

"Can you come by before that?"

"I wish I could, but I've got to finish up some stuff for my boss tonight. I promise I'll be there tomorrow."

Emily ended the call, wondering why Laura sounded so stressed.

Frank got into his car, leaning his head back onto the headrest. After meeting with the alcoholic support group and speaking with Devon, he'd hoped he could stop drinking. When he was at his apartment the previous night, he'd thought he could have just a little bit to drink, just enough to take the edge off his raw pain. But once he'd sipped the alcohol, he couldn't stop himself, and he fell asleep sloshed.

He called Devon this morning, telling him what had happened the night before. Devon had again stressed his group was a Christian support group and in order for Frank to give up the alcohol completely, he would need to surrender himself to Jesus. "That's the only way you can find the strength to quit."

He wondered how he could surrender his life to someone. He wanted to deal with things his way and live his life according to his own rules.

He drove to Emily's, pushing the thoughts from his mind. He slowed his car and parked in the driveway once he'd reached the farm. Frank got out of the car and walked toward the barn, smelling the odors of animals and hay. He eyed the black-and-white Holstein cows lined up in their stalls. Emily and a lanky teenager, whom he assumed was Jeremy or Darren, walked between the cows, milking four at a time. They worked together easily, and as the milk flowed through the pipes, the machines made a steady rhythm in the early evening heat.

Emily glanced up and smiled. "Frank, you're a little early."

She didn't seem to be too upset, and he didn't want to interrupt her milking routine. He gestured toward the bovines. "I don't want to interrupt you. I'll talk to you when you're finished."

He watched her, drinking in her presence like an ice-cold glass of lemonade on a hot day. The joy that radiated from her face was like a ray of sunshine.

Since the milking was done, she sent the teen to feed the cows before she rinsed her milking equipment in the adjoining room. He stood beside her at the sink as she performed the chore.

He touched her shoulder. "Are you ready to talk right now?" Hetouched the tendrils of her hair that escaped from her ponytail.

"Yes, we can talk now. What's happened with the audit for my farm? Mom sounded worried."

He sighed. "Your father had a gambling problem, Emily." He then repeated the information he'd relayed to Laura the previous day. Emily's mouth dropped open, and her eyes widened.

She backed away, shaking her head. "I don't believe you."

"I wish it wasn't true."

She stormed toward the teenager. "Finish cleaning the milking equipment and then feed the bull afterwards."

The lanky teen frowned as Emily yelled instructions to him like a drill sergeant.

Frank followed her as she practically ran to the house. "So, you're telling me that my father was a dishonest gambler?" She covered her quivering mouth. "That's not true! There's no way my father would place our farm in jeopardy."

Frank remained silent as she plopped onto the porch swing, unsure of how to comfort her.

She turned toward him, glaring. "So you're telling me that I could lose my farm, too?" Her large eyes filled with tears. "Is that what you're telling me?"

He ran his fingers over his head. "Yes, but—"

She looked away. "Are you sure you know what you're doing?"

The cold, hard edge to her voice frightened him. "What do you mean?"

"Were you sober the whole time you were auditing my farm?"

He clamped his mouth shut, shocked she would make such an implication. Taking a deep breath, he stood and walked away, unsure if she was serious or if she just needed an excuse because she didn't want to believe the truth about her father.

CHAPTER 12

EMILY WATCHED FRANK return to his car, and her heart pulsed with anger. She almost called him back, shocked at the words that had tumbled from her mouth. Shaking her head, she turned away from the accountant, staring at the corn and silos in the distance.

She wiped her tears away. Her head hurt and she felt like she was going to throw up. Maybe she shouldn't have eaten that thick greasy cheeseburger and fries before she milked the cows. Rocking the swing in the warm breeze, she tried to digest Frank's bad news. She jumped when Darren stepped onto the porch. "Sorry, didn't mean to scare you." The teen studied her, his dark eyes full of concern. "Hey, are you okay, Miss Emily?"

She sniffed. "There's so much going on right now." When he made no attempt to leave, she focused on him. "Did you need something?"

He nodded, his short braids swinging. "Yes, it's payday. Remember?"

"Oh, yes." Once she had given him his pay and he'd left, she returned to the porch swing.

Kelly pulled into the driveway and sauntered onto the porch as it started to get dark, still wearing her business suit and high heels. She plopped onto the swing beside Emily. "I was on my way home from work, and I thought I'd stop by." She peered into Emily's face. "What's wrong?"

Emily stared at the porch ceiling. "I can't even talk about it."

"You look zonked." She grabbed Emily's hand. "Come on inside."

Kelly fixed some peppermint tea and placed a plate of Emily's homemade milk chocolate candy on the table. "Have something to drink or eat. You look awful."

Emily's stomach roiled, and she pushed the tea away.

"Em, drink the tea. Maybe it will help calm you down." After taking several deep breaths, she sipped the tea as Kelly sat at the table with her. Kelly broke off a piece of chocolate and ate it. "Now, tell me what's wrong." She helped herself to more candy while she waited for Emily to begin.

"Frank said some terrible things about my father." Her voice sounded hoarse.

"What did he say?"

Emily could barely speak as she told her friend about Frank's accusations against her dad.

"Have you called Laura?"

"No, not yet. My mom did call me this morning, but I was out milking the cows. She left a message and said Becky and the baby are doing fine." She blew air through her lips. "I just don't know what to do. I don't know what to believe. And do you know what the worst part of it is?"

"What's that?"

"I asked if Frank was sober the entire time he was doing the audit."

Kelly dropped the chocolate she was eating and grabbed Emily's hand. "Em, I can't believe you said that."

Emily moaned. "Frank looked so hurt when I said it."

"Maybe you should apologize to him."

"I probably should. I just got so mad when he said those things. I was angry, and I said the first thing that came to my mind."

"Did you know he's been attending Devon Crandall's alcoholic support group?"

Emily stared at her friend. "I told him to talk to Devon, and he told me he'd tried to go to a meeting but he chickened out."

"Well, I heard through the church grapevine that he's been attending. Maybe he's trying to give up the alcohol, Em."

Emily's mouth quivered. "Oh no. What if my insensitive comment makes him go home and drink?" She closed her eyes. "Kelly, I feel so bad. I just. . ."

Kelly rushed over to her friend. "Give him some time to cool off. I'm sure he knew you didn't mean it."

Emily sniffed. "All those things he said about Daddy—I just can't believe them. I just can't."

Kelly left and returned with some pills. "I found that prescription you filled for your sleeping pills right after your father died. Here's two. Why don't you take them and get a good night's sleep?"

Emily accepted the pills and took them. She found she just couldn't talk any longer after Kelly had taken her exit and the medicine settled into her body. Her muscles relaxed, and she soon stumbled up the stairs to her bedroom. For the first time in her whole farming career, she fell asleep wearing the same clothes she wore to milk the cows.

Frank slammed the door to the accounting office building on Pratt Street. He stood on the corner, gazing at the buildings in the distance. Late evening tourists and shoppers walked by, their arms heavy with colorful store bags. He pulled off his tie, hating the managerial meeting that had occurred that day in the main office. His firm required all upper-level managers to wear business attire to these meetings, and he wasn't in the mood to wear his suit today. His boss had also called him into his office, informing him that he'd appeared irritable and cranky lately and he wondered if something was wrong. Frank couldn't admit that he needed a drink—badly. Emily's comment the previous evening had haunted him all night, and he had almost drunk some of his favorite scotch to dull the pain. He'd finally dumped the scotch down the toilet before tossing and turning most of the night.

Once he got into the car, he dropped his head back on the seat, groaning. "Oh God, I feel so bad right now." He started his car and pulled out of the lot. Forty minutes later, he pulled into a parking space at Dairy Christian Church, feeling a desperate need to meet with the alcoholic support group. He gazed at his Bible, still sitting on the passenger side of the car. Questions about God, life, and salvation filled his mind like unwanted weeds in a garden.

After walking into the practically deserted building, he entered the meeting room for the support group. During the meeting, he spoke of Emily's comment the previous evening and about how it had filled him with shame.

"Why were you ashamed?" asked one of the female attendees.

"Even though I was sober the whole time I was doing the audit, I could see myself getting to the point where I could have been drinking during the day." He went on to say that since he'd started drinking after his wife died, he noticed the amount of alcohol he consumed nightly had increased. "I've been waking up with bad headaches; sometimes I vomit."

Once the rest of the attendees had sprinkled in their words of wisdom and told of their weekly trials, Devon invited everybody to stand and join hands as they closed with a prayer. When the meeting was over, Frank pulled Devon aside. "I wanted to talk to you about something, Devon."

Devon invited him to return to his seat. Devon peered at him. "You look upset."

His wise, kind eyes bored into Frank.

"My addiction is really starting to bother me."

"I know it is. You're feeling guilty right now. I can tell." Devon's voice softened. "You know what you need to do. You need to surrender yourself to God."

"But that's so hard to do. My wife surrendered her life to God, but now she's dead."

"Her body is dead, but her spirit lives on. She's with Jesus right now, and you need to stop focusing on earthly life so much." He looked at Frank for a few seconds. "You know, Frank, I never did tell you my testimony. There's so much about me that I haven't had the chance to tell you yet." He checked his watch. "Are you in a hurry to leave?"

Frank dreaded the return to his empty apartment where thoughts of drinking continued to consume him. "No, I'm in no hurry."

They sat back down, and Devon began his

testimony. "I grew up in a home where alcohol flowed like water."

Frank frowned. "Do you mean both of your parents drank?"

Devon nodded. "My brother and I knew how wine and beer tasted before we even started kindergarten."

Frank gasped, shocked. "Your parents gave you booze?"

"No, they didn't give it to us directly. They were just irresponsible about how they left it around the house. My brother and I could get into the alcohol and drink it. We hated the taste but discovered we could water it down and drink it. It made us feel grown up."

"Your parents never knew what you did?"

"Since both of my parents drank so frequently, they didn't realize what was happening. Steve—that's my brother—and I grew up thinking it was okay to drink and get sloshed. Although our father was an alcoholic, he was always quoting scripture, saying Jesus died for our sins and that it was okay that he was getting drunk every night because God had already forgiven him for that. Steve and I grew up with the philosophy that we could do what we wanted as far as drinking was concerned because it was what we'd been hearing all our lives."

What a life. Just plain awful. He just couldn't imagine having parents like that. His parents were far from perfect, but, they'd never would have allowed him and Trish to nip into booze like that. He really wanted to know what had changed in Devon's life to make him quit drinking. "So, what changed your mind?"

"Steve and I were in the car with our father, and he was very drunk. He almost fell asleep at the wheel, and the car swerved into a ditch." He looked at the wall for a few seconds. "None of us were hurt, but at that point, I could see my dad's philosophy about being drunk was skewed. However, I was almost sixteen, and I was used to drinking whenever I wanted."

"Did your father continue drinking after the accident?"

"Not right away. He sobered up for a month or so, but before long, he was hitting the bottle as hard as ever. My mother's drinking was just as bad, and as I got ready to graduate from high school, I found that I wasn't happy unless I was drinking. From the type of household I was raised in, I thought the way I felt and handled things was normal. What really made me change my life was when my brother died from a drunk driving accident."

"Devon, I'm sorry." He patted the older man's shoulder. He gulped. This was a lot to process. He felt bad for Devon – that must've been hard losing his brother. He thought about Trish – how would he react if she'd died so tragically? He loved his sister – he hardly voiced it to her, but he did. As annoying as she was, he couldn't imagine his life without her in it. "I imagine that might've been one of the hardest things you've ever had to go through."

Devon nodded and wiped his wet eyes. "Losing my brother was the hardest thing I'd ever been through, and his death spurred me to look at myself emotionally and spiritually."

"What did you do?"

"Although I'd been raised by a father who quoted scripture all the time, I realized that I'd never really studied the Bible for myself, word for word, to see what God really said we should do to live a life that was pleasing to Him. I was twenty years old at the time, and I searched around until I found a small church where I felt comfortable. I began studying the scriptures with other believers until I finally proclaimed Christ as my Savior. My father died of liver disease because of his heavy drinking when I was twenty-five, but he'd learned to control his drinking after Steve died. My mom, dad, and I all found the Lord after Steve's death, and I make sure when I convince people to accept Christ that they hear about what I went through as I searched for the Lord."

Devon's testimony sank deeply into Frank's heart, and he thought about Devon Crandall's advice as he drove home that night.

CHAPTER 13

THE FOLLOWING SATURDAY, Frank struggled to open his eyes. He swallowed, thinking about his tormented night. Emily's accusation still felt like a punch in the gut. He'd actually made it through the day without a drink, and he'd been on the phone with Devon last night for a whole hour. The urge for a drink consumed him, and he shuffled over to the coffee pot, making a large pot of the steaming brew. He sipped the coffee, recalling Devon's advice. "Son, you need to accept the Lord. Fall down on your knees and accept Him. Surrender your life to Him. That's the only way you can give up the drink."

The ringing telephone interrupted his musings, and he jumped. Groaning, he picked up the receiver. "Hello."

"Frank? It's Emily." Her smooth, sweet voice reminded him of silk. He relished the pleasure of hearing her speak.

"Emily? I'm surprised you called."

"I wanted to apologize for what happened the other day. I shouldn't have said those things to you."

He tried to think of the right words to say. The hurt from her accusation had pierced through him like a lightning bolt; still, he knew she was justified in her assumption, even though it was wrong. "I. . .can I see you sometime today? I wanted to talk to you about something."

"You haven't had anything to drink today, have you? I don't want you to drive over here if you've been drinking. I know you're trying to quit. . ."

"It's hard to stop completely."

She sighed. "That's what I've heard. That's why I want to make sure you're okay. I just don't want you driving over here if you're drinking. I worry about you, Frank."

"You don't have to worry about me. Remember I told you that I only drink at night after I get home."

They agreed to meet for dinner, and Emily offered to meet Frank in Baltimore, but he refused, telling her that he would pick her up.

Darren showed up for work that evening, so after they milked the cows and fed them, she strolled toward the house as the conversation she'd had with Frank that morning still played in her mind. After removing her barn boots, she entered her home and went upstairs to take a long, hot shower, still contemplating the fate of her farm. After showering, she sprayed perfume over her skin before pulling her hair back into a ponytail. Sporting faded jeans and a large red T-shirt, she was more than ready to meet with Frank to discuss her farm.

The crunch of gravel signaled the approach of Frank's car. Emily bounded down the stairs and exited the house into the humid night. The sun was just beginning to set, and the sky was pink and bright orange. Her heart skipped a beat when he touched her arm.

"It's nice to see you again."

She nodded. "It's good to see you, too."

They were soon in his Lexus, taking the forty-minute drive toward downtown Baltimore. While driving, he told her about his recent conversations with Mark and how Trish still worried about the boy's erratic behavior. "I just wish his father would take a more active role in his life." Emily was touched that Frank was so worried about his nephew. He spoke about it so frequently that he almost seemed like a father instead of an uncle.

He gestured toward a restaurant when they arrived in Baltimore. "Do you mind if we go to the M&S Grill?"

"That sounds good."

They entered the spacious restaurant, and she wondered why Frank had brought his briefcase with him. Their server approached. "We'd like an outside table," Frank informed the server.

They ordered sodas when they were seated, and before the server could leave, Frank asked Emily a question. "Do you mind if I order for both of us?"

Food was the last thing on her mind. "I don't mind."

He ordered the flounder stuffed with crab imperial for both of them. "I've been doing a lot of eating out since I've been here. They make the best stuffed flounder."

His leg jiggled. She touched his hand. "Are you okay?"

He sighed, looking toward the water. Boats bobbed in the hot breeze, and if there weren't so many issues between them, Emily could imagine having a pleasant time with Frank this evening.

His dark, mesmerizing eyes looked tortured. "No, I'm not okay. I need a drink."

She took a deep breath before voicing her next question. "Have you stopped drinking?"

"Sort of."

She frowned, still touching his hand. "What do you mean?"

"Well, I got drunk a few nights ago."

"Have you had a drink since?"

"No."

"Well, that's good then. You're on the right track." She tried to remain positive. Groups of teenagers strolled down the sidewalk, laughing as they passed on the busy pavement. "Has Devon Crandall been helping you?"

"Yes, I've been speaking to Devon over the last few weeks. He's a nice guy. He's caring."

"Yes, Devon's been through a lot. Did he share his testimony with you?"

"Yes, but he says I need to accept Christ if I want to find the strength to quit drinking completely."

"He's right. You've got to give God a chance." He ran his fingers over his short hair. "I know what your problem is." He remained silent. "You just like having complete control over your life."

His mouth hardened. "Yeah, so what?"

She shook her head. "But you're not controlling your life. The alcohol is." He winced, looking away. She squeezed his hand. "Frank, you can't control your life. You've got to let God help you."

They silently sipped their drinks for a few seconds before she gestured toward his briefcase. "Why did you bring that?"

Sighing, he removed a thick stack of cream-colored paper. "Emily, here's what I wanted to discuss with you."

He went through former tax returns and worksheets, explaining things to Emily. "Bottom line, you owe the IRS this amount of money." He pointed to a large figure on the paper.

Emily gasped. She had her small savings that she'd been hoarding for her future trip to Tahiti. But, the amount she'd saved wasn't nearly enough money to pay the IRS.

Their flounder arrived, but she had lost her appetite. The server left their food at the side of the table since they were still looking through Frank's papers. "Does this mean that if Laura and I don't pay this back, we'll lose the farm?"

Frank slowly nodded. "You could lose your farm." He quickly squeezed her hand. "But, there are ways to get around this that might work."

Emily blinked, still trying to drink in all the information. "Like what?"

He opened his napkin, avoiding her intense gaze. "I've already contacted the IRS—"

Her mouth dropped open. "You already reported my father?"

Grabbing her hand, he rubbed her palm, and her anger disappeared like a calm sea after a raging storm. "You know I wouldn't report your father to the IRS without clearing it with you or Laura first." He sighed, still holding her hand. "I just contacted them, without giving any personal information, and asked how I could advise a client about their situation. I didn't give the name of you or your family." He looked at her directly. "You could possibly get a bank loan, but I doubt it since your father already has that farm mortgaged to the brim."

Emily continued to stare at Frank. "Do you have any other suggestions?"

Frank released her hand. Without answering her question, he pulled their plates from the side of the table, placing one in front of Emily and one in front of himself. He took a large bite of his flounder. She wondered how he could eat at a time like this and why he wouldn't answer her question.

She looked at her plate. The delicate white fish made her stomach churn.

Taking her fork, she took a small bite.

Frank sipped his Coke. "Emily, I don't know how you feel about this."

"About what?" She put her fork aside, giving him her full attention.

"Well, I could give you the resources so your farm won't be confiscated."

She gasped. "I can't accept that kind of money from you."

He took another sip of Coke. "It could be a loan."

Gritting her teeth, she gazed toward the Chesapeake Bay. "I don't know if we could pay you back."

"Don't worry about that yet. I just want to do what I can so that you won't lose your farm." She stared at his bent head as he ate.

"Why would you do this for me?"

He didn't respond, and she wondered why he refused to look at her. "Frank?" She placed her hand over his arm, forcing him to stop eating his meal.

"I. . .I just want to do this."

She looked at the patrons at the surrounding tables eating their evening meals, still trying to comprehend. "But I still don't understand. . ."

"I just want to help out a friend. What's wrong with that?"

She stared at him, still trying to decipher his actions. She was unsure of what to say. Her deep feelings for Frank rushed through her, but she knew that if she was indebted to him, it would make their situation sticky. She pushed the papers toward him. "I can't talk about this anymore."

Once Frank dropped her off, Emily's mind was spinning. She'd called Laura, but she was in the midst of serving dinner to Becky's family, and there was chaos in the background. "Mom, call me back later tonight when you get a chance. It's okay if you wake me up." Since there was a three-hour time difference, Emily didn't want Laura to hesitate about calling her if she thought she was going to wake her.

She sat on the couch in the dark living room and didn't realize she'd fallen asleep until the phone awakened her. She lifted the receiver. "Hello."

"Hey, Emily. It's Kelly."

"And Christine. Kelly has us on three-way."

"Hi, guys." Emily cleared her throat, still trying to clear her sleep-clogged brain.

"You sound like you're asleep," said Christine. "Emily, what's been going on with you?"

Emily stood. "Hold on, my throat is dry. Let me get a glass of water." After filling a glass, she guzzled the cold liquid down, relieving her parched throat. When she sat back down, she told Kelly and Christine about her conversation with Frank.

"He offered you that money because he loves you." Kelly told her opinion.

Emily wondered if Kelly was telling the truth. "Loves me? Frank doesn't love me. He's never told me this."

Christine interjected. "I haven't had a serious relationship in years, but from my limited experience, love is very complicated."

Emily clutched the receiver. "How do you guys know Frank loves me?"

Kelly sighed. "You should see the way he stares at you in church! He loves you, girl. I don't know why he hasn't told you yet, but I'm sure he'll tell you eventually."

"I don't think he loves me."

"Yes, he loves you, Emily," Christine said. "Now stop being so hardheaded about it and accept it for what it is."

They talked for a few more minutes before

finally saying good night. But her friends' words rang in her ears as she trudged up the stairs to get ready for bed.

CHAPTER 14

FRANK STRUGGLED THROUGH life the next few weeks. The urge to drink washed through him in waves, and he spoke to Devon daily. The older man had advised him to take it one day at a time. "That way your whole situation won't seem so hopeless," he'd said.

Emily filtered through his mind constantly, and he still wanted her to accept his offer of help for her farm. When his boss had called him into his office again, he'd reminded Frank that his temporary venture to start up the farm and ranch accounting division of their company had come to an end. "You've done an awe- some job, and you've worked a tremendous amount of overtime. Would you like to stay as part of the farm and ranch division here in Baltimore, or would you rather return to Chicago? The choice is yours." The partnership was still not mentioned and with his present state of mind, he decided not to mention it. He'd been tired, struggling not to take a drink and a few times he'd been cranky, snapping at his coworkers.

He walked along the grounds of the Cylburn Arboretum in Baltimore City, his boss's words running through his mind like a speeding train. Since Frank had agreed that it was best he return to Chicago, his boss had hired a replacement for him. The company event at the Arboretum was a threefold celebration: Frank's going-away celebration, the new hire's welcome party, and a celebration of the success of their new division.

His company had rented a room on the first floor of the building, and when his coworkers drank glasses of champagne, Frank thought he would lose his mind. He'd frowned when the alcoholic beverage was popped open by a catering employee. As the beige-colored liquid was poured into glass flutes, his boss must have noted his reaction when he'd approached him. "Don't frown so much, Franklin. We're off the clock now, so we can have a drink to celebrate our success. We do the same thing when we have our Christmas party every year."

Frank had nodded, heat rushing through him. His boss had placed his hand on Frank's arm. "You look like you could use a drink. Let me get you a glass."

Frank had shaken his head. "No. I'm not feeling too good right now. I think I'll go for a walk on the grounds." He'd practically fled the large mansion and onto the landscaped property. The warm sun soothed him as he walked farther away from the building. He finally found a bench outside in the massive garden. Colorful butterflies fluttered above the large expanse of flowers. The rainbow of blooms created a carpet of color, surrounding him with their scent. The leaves on the nearby trees were turning color, hinting at the autumn weather that was coming soon. "Lord, what am I going to do?"

He continued to take pleasure in his surroundings as thoughts filtered through his brain. He recalled Devon's advice. "Give the Lord a chance, son. That's about all you can do to keep the alcohol away." Emily's sweet face came to mind, and he recalled her words of wisdom as they'd shared dinner together. "Frank, you can't control your life. You've got to let God help you."

He recalled Julie's happiness once she'd accepted Jesus into her life. Tears stained his cheeks as a black-and-yellow butterfly hovered around his bench. He wiped his eyes, realizing he couldn't control his life on his own anymore. He needed help—in the worst way. "Lord, help me. I'm a sinner; please help me, Lord." His shoulders shook as he cried and accepted God's grace for his sins.

A few days later when Emily returned home from running errands, she was shocked to see

Frank's Lexus parked in her driveway. He'd been to church the last couple of Sundays but had rushed off before she had a chance to speak with him. Her farm's fate weighed upon her mind, and she realized that once Laura returned, they would need to sit down and decide what to do about the back taxes owed on their property.

She exited her truck, holding several bags of purchases. Frank sat on her screened-in porch, waiting for her. His trusty leather briefcase stood upright on the floor, and she wondered why he had brought it with him. They gazed at each other, silent.

"Hi," he finally greeted. The bags grew heavy in her arms, and she almost dropped them before Frank came to her rescue. "Here, let me help you with those."

"Thanks." They carried the bags into the house and placed them on the table.

He touched her shoulder. "You look tired. Are you okay?"

"It's been a rough day."

"Did something happen?"

She dropped her purse on the table. "Yes, the inspector showed up this morning." Emily had once to Frank how the inspector would show up unannounced periodically, making sure their dairy farm fit the government's standards.

"Did he find anything wrong?"

"No, but he sure tried. He was here long

enough, poking around. I just wanted him to leave."

"Did anything else happen?"

"Thunderbolt got out."

"Huh?"

"Thunderbolt is one of the cows. She's feisty and fast. She's new to the milking herd, and when Jeremy and I were letting the cows out to graze this morning, Thunderbolt ran right past us." She pouted. "It was awful. We ran into the road to get her back. It took us a whole hour to coax her back to the farm, and she held up traffic."

He glanced around the silent house. "Is Laura here?"

She placed a carton of milk in the refrigerator. "No, she's still in California."

"When will she be back?"

Emily sat, suddenly too weary to put the rest of the groceries away. "She'll be back next week. She has to start working at the cafeteria again because school's already started. She called the school, and they said she could start a couple of weeks late. The C-section is about healed, and Becky's getting used to the baby's constant demands." She talked about her stepsister's plight for a few minutes before she realized she was babbling. "I know you didn't come here to get an update on Becky's health."

"No, I didn't." Sunlight streamed into the bright, airy kitchen, highlighting Frank's pleasant features. Emily realized she could just sit and stare at this man forever. She pushed the thought from her mind, realizing there was little hope for them to have a relationship. He lifted his briefcase, placing it on the table. Snapping the gold locks open, he removed a sheaf of papers. "You never took the final paperwork for the audit of your farm." He placed the cream-colored papers on the table.

"Thanks."

"As soon as I leave, I want you to promise me you'll look through all this."

She gestured toward the papers. "I'll get to it eventually."

He shook his head. "Please promise me you'll at least glance through them after I've left."

His dark eyes were full of sadness when he gazed at her, and she wondered if everything was okay. "I promise." When silence weighed heavily in the kitchen again, she spoke. "You just came to bring me the papers?"

He sighed when he sat. He ran his fingers over his short dark hair, and the familiar gesture warmed her heart. "No, that's not the only reason I came." He paused. "I'm going back to Chicago."

Her heart stopped. "You're kidding."

"I wouldn't kid about this, sweetheart."

"But. . .but why?"

"I told you that I was initially here for a temporary time."

"You can't stay?"

He shook his head. "I'd like to but. . ." He balled his hands into fists. "I have to make things right with my folks." He took a deep breath. "I don't think I have much time left, so I have to go home."

"Did something happen with your parents?"

"Trish called me a few hours ago. My dad has had a stroke."

She grabbed his hand. "Frank, I'm so sorry. Will he be okay?"

"No, the doctors don't expect him to live long. I have to go home."

She patted his shoulder. "Of course, you do. I'll be praying for you and your family." So many questions littered her brain like unwanted weeds in a garden. Would Frank be coming back? Would this be the last time she'd see him? Would he ever accept Christ?

"I don't know when I'll be strong enough to come back."

She took his hand again. "Frank, please give God a chance. Just come to Him as you are, and He'll accept you. He'll give you the strength to get you through anything. You don't have to fix yourself before you come to Jesus."

"I've given up alcohol for a short time, and it's been terrible." He told her about his acceptance of Christ at the Cylburn Arboretum. "Emily, I'm a sinner in the worst way. Even before my father had a stroke, I was still planning on going to Chicago."

His words surprised her, and she realized they could find a way to make it work between them with the Lord's help. "Frank, we're all sinners. Although you say you've accepted Christ, it sounds like you're still harboring guilt. Jesus doesn't want us to feel guilty. Let Him take all that guilt and sadness off your shoulders. Jesus has already paid the price for all our sins. If you follow the Lord, that'll give you the strength you need."

"I'm a new Christian, and I'm still trying to make my life right. I don't know how long I can stay away from alcohol, even with the Lord on my side." With his father's predicament, he knew he'd find it hard not to drink. "It's unfair of me to want to be with you, knowing I'm so weak."

His words made her speechless. She stared at him, drinking him in, not knowing what to say or do. Soon he was beside her, and his lips touched hers in a brief, tender kiss. She didn't realize she was crying until Frank gave her a napkin from the dispenser on the table. "Are you coming back?"

"I don't know. I'd like to come back when I feel I'm no longer a threat."

"What do you mean?"

"I'm an alcoholic. You've never seen me when I'm drunk. It's not pleasant. It's not right for me to be with you if I turn back to the bottle again."

"We could try. With the Lord's help, we can make it work."

"I have faith, but I don't think my faith is as

strong as yours. I'm still praying about it, asking the Lord to lead me into doing the right things. I know He wants me to return to Chicago and spend some time with my dad since I don't know how long he will live." He glanced away for a few seconds. "My mother's always depended on my dad, and I think it'll break her if he dies." He looked at his watch. "I have to get going."

"So you're driving back?"

"Yes, I had a moving company come and take my stuff to Trish's house. She lives in a large home outside of Chicago, and I'll be staying with her until I've made other living arrangements. The movers left this morning, and Trish is expecting them."

"Can we at least keep in touch? I'd like to know how your father is doing." She also wanted to know how Frank was doing.

"Yes, I'd like that."

She wanted to know if he wanted her to wait for him, but she couldn't bring herself to voice those words. He gestured toward the papers before removing his car keys from the pocket of his jeans. "Be sure to keep your promise to me and read those papers after I leave?"

She nodded, still speechless. The screen door banged shut when he left, and gravel crunched beneath his tires as he drove away from the farm.

She watched Frank's burgundy Lexus until it disappeared from view. She then took the stack of papers he'd left and sat on the porch.

The letter was from Franklin Reese, CPA, stating the validity of the financial papers and the results of his audit. Emily didn't understand most of the terms and language, but she recognized a lot of the stuff Frank had shown her at the restaurant the other day. The papers outlined the violations her father had committed and recommended going to the IRS with a payment plan to repay the back taxes. He'd also placed a side note, stating that his replacement, Melvin Sparks, could be entrusted to contact the IRS on their behalf and with filing the amended returns. If they repaid the money, he doubted there would be a lot of trouble from the government agency.

There was also a bill enclosed, noting Frank's hours, but the bill was marked

Paid in Full. Emily fingered the cream-colored stationery, shocked that they did not have to pay for Frank's labor.

Frank had also enclosed a check for enough money to cover the balance due to the IRS. She hugged the envelope to her chest. "Oh, Daddy, why did you have to die? Why did you have to be so dishonest?" She sniffed, crying tears of grief. "Lord, what am I supposed to do now? Daddy's dead, Frank is gone, and Laura won't be back for a while. I feel so lost and alone, Lord. Please help me find some peace."

After much prayer, thought, and deliberation,

Emily decided to accept Frank's gift. The day she deposited the funds, she fell on her knees, saying a prayer to God.

CHAPTER 15

AS THE MONTHS passed following Frank's departure, Emily found that her thoughts of Frank continued to haunt her. He e-mailed her a few times, and she knew his father had eventually died. She'd wanted to call him, but she wasn't sure if he wanted to speak with her. She moped about the house, did farm chores, and helped their hired workers harvest the corn. Kelly and Christine came over often, and they called periodically, but her friends couldn't cheer her up.

Laura had been concerned about her since Frank had left. Laura had a friend who owned a vacation beach house in Virginia Beach. After making arrangements for Jeremy and Darren to do the milking for a few days, Emily and Laura went to the beach house for an extended weekend of relaxation. They spent a lot of time sitting outside staring at the beach. Fishing boats bobbled in the cool water. Since it was autumn, the beach water was too cool for swimming. Emily took advantage of the using the indoor pool at the nearby Virginia Beach Community Center. She took a good long swim at the indoor pool every morning and evening.

After her swim, Laura always had a big tasty meal, waiting to be consumed. Emily made a big pan of her milk chocolate candy with nuts. On their last day of vacation, they sat on the deck of the beach house. Laura had brewed a huge pot of hazelnut coffee and served it up in huge beach-themed mugs. She placed a plate of Emily's candy on the table.

Emily closed her eyes, snuggled in her light jacket, leaning back enjoying the early afternoon sunshine. The brilliant sunlight spilled into the space as they snacked on candy and sipped coffee. "Mom, are you glad to be back in Dairy?"

Laura shrugged. "I miss your father. But it is nice to be back and into a routine again. I like working at the school cafeteria and seeing the kids every day." A wistful look crossed her face as she stirred her coffee.

"Mom, what's wrong? You've been acting like something's been on your mind since you returned from Becky's."

Laura shrugged. "It's nothing I feel like talking about right now."

Emily tasted another bite of candy, figuring Laura would tell her what was on her mind when she was ready. She relished the amazing view of the ocean.

"You still saving up for your beach trip to Tahiti, Emily?"

"No, I stopped doing that."

"Honey, don't. I know how much you love beaches."

Emily shook her head. "But, what about Frank? The money I have saved up was enough for a partial repayment to him. We owe him a lot of money." She took a deep breath. "Instead of putting my extra money into a savings account for my trip, I'm going to start paying Frank back."

"Emily, don't worry about that. Frank's a good, kindhearted man. I'm sure he'll accept the payment whenever we can manage to give it to him." Laura sampled some candy.

"Laura, no, this is something I have to do. Frank..it was nice that he helped us. He's kindhearted and thoughtful and..well…I just don't want to take advantage of him. We owe him that money so, I'm going to give it back to him, even if it takes me several years, I plan on paying him back."

"I understand, Emily. I'll help when I can. I get my salary as a lunch lady at the school. It's not much but…" she shrugged. "I live at the farm too and I should help you."

"Thanks, Mom."

"You think about Frank a lot, don't you?"

Emily placed her cup on the table. "How did you know?"

"I can always tell when you're thinking about

him." They sat in silence for a few moments, watching a few seagulls glide through the sky.

"I was just thinking about how I got to know him while he was here." She told Laura about the close bond he shared with his nephew and about how he used to mentor teens at the rec center in Chicago. Emily thought he'd make a great father but didn't want to voice that opinion. If she dwelled on that too much, it would just make her long for something that might never happen.

"You know, you've been through a lot lately." Emily shrugged, sipping her hot drink. "I guess so. But spending time away here in Virginia Beach is nice. I don't want to go back home today."

"I agree. Actually, I have a suggestion to make."

"What's that?"

"I wondered if you wanted to go and visit your cousin Monica in Ocean City for a week."

"But, Mom, we're taking a break right now."

Laura shooed the comment away. "We're only here for a few days. You just said you weren't ready to leave. You need a week or so away from the farm."

"But, who will do the milking?"

"I've already spoken to some people, and we have enough extra help so that you can go on a vacation. You need it. When I was in Florida following Paul's death, it did wonders for my mental health."

"I don't know." She found some solace just spending time with the animals each day.

Her stepmother touched her hand. "You've been moody lately, and I know Frank really hurt your feelings when he left. I think a change in scenery may help you out of your mood."

When Emily finished her coffee, she told Laura she would call and check with Monica. If she said it was okay, she'd take her vacation the following week. Maybe the change in scenery was what she needed.

The following week, Emily arrived at her cousin's house. Monica and her husband, John, welcomed her into their home. She also got a chance to visit with Monica's sister, Gina, and Scotty, Gina's blind nine-year-old son. The child read a lot of braille books and magazines, and Monica confided how Scotty's educational needs were what brought her together with John. She'd explained that John was Scotty's tutor, and that was how they'd met.

One day, following a fun-filled Saturday of sightseeing in Ocean City, while Scotty, John and Gina took a walk, Emily and Monica sat on lawn chairs on the cold shore of the of the beach. Earlier, John had built a bonfire and the warmth felt good on this frigid evening. The cold breeze blew. Seeing the water lap onto the shore soothed her. She snuggled beneath the large beach blanket that they were sharing. She focused on her cousin.

"Monica, I noticed that John is very affectionate toward you."

Monica chuckled. "Yes, he is. I just never thought I'd fall so deeply in love."

"I'm sorry I missed your wedding last year. Dad had the flu, and I had to stay and take care of the farm."

Monica smiled. "That's okay." She removed her phone from her purse. "Let me show you our wedding pictures." She found the picture album on her phone before handing the phone to Emily.

Emily slowly scrolled through the pics, taking time to admire each one. "These are beautiful."

"Thanks." Once she had looked at all the pictures, Monica told Emily some news. "I'm pregnant."

Emily's heart filled with joy. "You're kidding."

"Nope! We can hardly wait."

She hugged her cousin. "I'm so happy for both of you; I really am." When they broke their embrace, tears slipped from Emily's eyes, and Monica handed her a tissue.

She touched Emily's shoulder. "Cousin, why are you so sad?"

Emily wondered if Monica would truly understand her problems, but she had to tell Monica all that had happened since her father's death. She closed her eyes for a few seconds, enjoying the sound of the water lapping onto the shore. Once she'd calmed down, she eyed Monica. "I just can't believe my father was a gambler." She told her about Frank, his drinking, his salvation, and his sudden disappearance from her life. "He's e-mailed me a few times, but I miss him like crazy."

"Why do you like him so much?"

"He's kind, he's caring, he's conscientious, and I like being with him. I like being around him. I hated his drinking, and the fact that he was unsaved really bothered me. Now that he's saved, I'd hoped we could work things out. But it looks like I was wrong. I just wish he wasn't afraid of turning into an alcoholic again, but I can't make his desire to drink go away."

"Does he still talk to you? Other than the e-mails?"

"He doesn't call me, but he is in Chicago right now, and I know his father died. We don't have constant contact, just an occasional e-mail. He's texted me a couple of times, too."

"Have you thought about calling him?"

"No. I sense he doesn't want to talk to me." Another thought occurred to her. "You know, maybe he doesn't like me very much."

"He saved your farm for you. I think he likes you a lot, but he's working through his issues right now."

She shook her head. "No. There's no hope for us."

"Girl, where's your faith? If the Lord allowed John and me to be together, then I know there's hope for you and Frank."

"What do you mean?"

Monica glanced at her wedding pics. "John was an agnostic."

"Really? I didn't know that."

"Yeah. He didn't even know if he believed God existed. When he first started tutoring my nephew, we shared an instant attraction, but I knew there was no hope for us because of his beliefs."

"But he accepted Jesus," Emily guessed.

"He sure did. So, since God saw fit to bring John and I together, then He might see fit to bring you together with Frank."

"I just wish I could get Frank off my mind."

"Are you involved in any of the ministries at your church?" Emily told her about the outreach ministry. "Is there a singles group at your church?"

"There's one that started just shortly after Frank left. Kelly, Christine, and I joined, but I just haven't felt like going to the meetings. Why do you ask?"

"It might be more fun and fulfilling to hang out with other Christian singles. I remember when I was in the singles group at my church a long time ago, I never met anybody to date, but I had a good time. We'd have fun and fellowship time, and we'd go bowling, out to dinner, out to the movies." Monica shrugged. "It was fun, and it gave me something to do. Also, what do you like to do in your spare time besides work on your dairy farm?"

"Years ago, I used to read novels, but it's something I just stopped doing."

"Well, why don't you start doing that again? If I recall, during the winter you don't have as much to do on your farm as you do during the summer months since you're not harvesting any crops or baling hay. If you're worried about spending a lot of money on books, you could always go to the library or a used book store."

"So, you're saying that I need to keep myself busy and not worry about Frank so much?"

"Exactly. I certainly can't predict if he'll come back, but if it's the Lord's will, then Frank will come sweeping back to Dairy to be with you again. But if he doesn't come back, at least you'll be so occupied with your new activities that you'll barely notice. When I was pining after a man, another thing I did was get more acquainted with God. Why don't you try reading some more of the Word and focusing on God? I know it'd help."

"You make it sound so easy."

Monica touched Emily's shoulder. The flames from the bonfire highlighted her cousin's pretty face. "By no means is it easy. I'm not saying doing all these things will make Frank disappear from your mind, but it might help. I can honestly say that I know how you feel, but you just have to take it one day at a time and try and focus on yourself and God until you find out what Frank's going to do."

As both of them enjoyed the bonfire, Emily pondered Monica's advice for the rest of the evening.

CHAPTER 16

Four months later

"W-WOULD YOU L-L-LIKE another s-s-s-soda?" Cameron Jacobs held Emily's hand, leading her to their seats at the spring gospel concert. People milled about, trying to find their seats in the arena as several waited near the stage, eager for the performance to start.

"I'm fine, Cameron." She put her cold soda aside, no longer thirsty.

Emily continued to think about Frank periodically and wondered why he had only e-mailed and texted her a few times. She still clung to Monica's advice that Frank would find help for his issues and return to Baltimore County; however, as time passed, her prayers remained unanswered, and she wondered if maybe the Lord was nudging her to let go of her fantasy of being with Frank.

During the holiday season a few months ago, she'd mailed him a Christmas card. She'd hoped and prayed for a response, but she had only received Frank's silence.

She studied the arena. The gospel concert was one of her favorite yearly events. This year, however, the festive music failed to lift her spirits. Sighing, she ran her fingers through her hair.

"I like your new haircut, E–E–Emily. It l–l–looks good on you."

Emily smiled her thanks to Cameron, although "new" wouldn't describe her haircut. A short time after her visit to Monica, she felt the weight of her long, dark hair to be too much to handle. She'd visited her hairdresser and asked for a short, snazzy cut.

The band warmed up as Emily thought about the last four months of her life—about how she ended up coming to this gospel concert with Cameron.

Weeks following her visit with Monica, Cameron had asked her out yet again, so she finally relented and went out with the man. He was a person of strong faith, and she wondered if the Lord was trying to tell her that Cameron was the man she should pursue.

She knew when Frank was in town, he'd often talked to Cameron after church. Frank and Cameron had also gone to an Orioles game once. Heaven help her, the first question she'd asked Cameron when they'd started dating was if he'd ever heard from Frank.

Cameron's answer had been an emphatic *no*.

She never should've asked. Cameron had seemed a bit hurt that she'd boldly asked that question. It didn't take a genius to figure out that she still pined after her former accountant.

This was their fifth date, and so far, Emily felt nothing for Cameron except feelings of friendship. He barely crossed her mind throughout her day, and he didn't haunt her dreams, unlike Frank.

"E-E-Emily!" Emily snapped out of her reverie, gazing at Cameron's confused expression. "The concert is over."

"Oh, sorry." She smiled and stood, gathering her coat. Cameron helped her with her garment, and she watched several other members of the audience retrieve their things as they headed to the large parking lot.

They drove home in silence. Emily gazed at the brightly lit windows of the stores downtown. Huddling into her coat, she was eager to return home and finish reading the Christian cozy mystery novel she'd started earlier that week. When Cameron pulled into the lot, she noticed another car in her driveway.

"Are y-y-you and your m-mother expecting company tonight?"

Emily frowned at the unfamiliar car. "I don't think so. But sometimes people from the church will drop by and visit." She remained silent when Cameron rushed out of the car and opened her door for her.

He walked her to the bottom of her porch.

Emily sensed from the eager expression on Cameron's face that he was anticipating a good night kiss or an invitation inside for a piece of her milk chocolate candy. "Good night, Cam." She turned away and started toward the porch, not even giving him a chance to kiss her.

He stopped her with a question. "You d-d-don't like me very m-m-much, do y-y-you?"

She turned toward him again. "I think you're a nice man."

"N-n-nice? You don't like me the way you liked F-F-Frank. I saw the way you used to look at him in c-c-c-church."

Emily didn't want to hurt Cameron's feelings. "I think you're a strong, good man, and I admire your faith in God."

His shoulders drooped. "I w-w-w-won't ask you out anymore, E-E-Emily. I feel like I'm wasting my t-t-t-time."

She didn't want him to feel bad. "Cameron. Don't get mad."

"I'm not m-m-mad. It's just. . .whenever I'm with y-y-you, I feel like you're not with m-m-me."

She frowned, squinting at him in the darkness. "What do you mean?"

"Your mind is always on s-s-something. Half the time when I s-s-s-speak to you, I have to repeat myself. I almost get the f-f-feeling you can't wait for our dates to e-e-end."

Emily inwardly winced, hating that Cameron

could read her so easily. "I'm sorry, Cam." She held out her hand, not wanting things to end on a bad note. "We're still friends, right?"

He gave her a small smile, shaking her hand. "Yeah, we're still f-f-friends. I'll be seeing you when I come to get your m-m-milk tomorrow." He gestured toward the porch. "Since your house is d-d-dark and you don't recognize that c-c-car in your driveway, I'll just walk you to your d-d-door and make sure you get in o-o-okay."

"Thanks." His heavy footsteps followed her up the porch steps as she opened the creaky screen door. Cameron was right behind her as she tried to locate the door handle to the house in the darkness.

"Emily." A figure appeared, and Emily almost screamed when Cameron jumped on the person trespassing on their porch. Cameron and the trespasser landed on the floor, making a huge racket. "Get off me! Emily, it's me, Frank!"

"Oh my." Her voice trembled and her hands shook as she jerked the kitchen door open, turning on the light. The men stood simultaneously, Cameron glaring at Frank.

"Y-y-ou could have let Emily know you were on the porch instead of s-s-scaring her. E-Emily, do you want me to stay, or are you okay alone with h-him?" Cameron shot a look at Frank.

In spite of their shared conversations at church and enjoying a ball game together, looked like

Cameron was sore that Frank had shown up unexpectedly.

Frank grunted. "Hey, Cameron. Calm down. We can talk about this after church one day." Frank offered his hand and Cameron stared at his hand for a few seconds before shaking it. "I'm glad you made sure Emily made it to her door okay."

"N–no t–thanks needed."

"I'm fine, Cameron. Thanks for seeing me to my door."

"I–I j–just said no t–thanks n–needed." Cameron nodded, clomped down the stairs to his car and sprinted away in his car so quickly that his headlights disappeared in a couple of seconds as he rounded the corner.

Her fright subsided when she entered the kitchen, and she quickly disarmed their recently installed burglar alarm before beckoning Frank inside. Her heart was pounding so hard, she felt it would pop out of her chest.

Suddenly, Frank was bathed in the warm glow of the kitchen light. He'd changed. He removed his leather jacket, and her breathing intensified when she looked up into his cocoa brown eyes. She peered at his face, which now sprouted a thick beard and mustache.

"Frank, I. . . Why are you here?" Her voice shook as she slowly sat at the kitchen table.

He shrugged, continuing to stare. "I came to

see you. Laura wasn't home, so I decided to wait for you on the porch. Didn't you notice my car outside?"

Emily nodded. Her legs felt weightless as blood rushed to her head. "It's not the same car you had ...you had when you left."

He chuckled. "That's right. I'd forgotten that you haven't seen my new car."

She shrugged. "When I saw your car, I just figured we had a visitor. I don't know where Laura is." She spotted the note on the refrigerator. Emily read the note, which said that her stepmother was going to be spending the night with a troubled church member. "Laura won't be home tonight. She's been really busy since she joined the church's outreach program." She placed the note on the table.

"I don't recall Laura being in the outreach ministry before. I thought you were a part of that ministry."

She didn't feel like talking about church activities. But she forced herself to comment on Frank's observation. "I decided to stop being in that ministry, and my stepmother offered to take my place." She shrugged. "I had other ministries I wanted to be involved with." She pointed to the pile of books in the corner of the kitchen. "I've been reading some good Christian novels lately, and I've started a book club at my church. I've also been involved with the singles ministry, too. These things keep me busy. I still have a lot of chores to do on the farm, but not nearly as many as during the summertime."

"How're things on the farm? How's your herd of cows doing?"

Emily gave him a quick rundown on all that had happened with her farm animals since he'd left. She kept talking before she finally stopped herself, not wanting to act like things were okay between them. "Are you here visiting?" she asked abruptly.

"Emily, I'm back in Dairy for good now." Emily stared at Frank, wondering if this was another dream. "A lot has happened to me over the last six months."

She listened to him, still finding it hard to believe he was in her kitchen, talking as if they'd just seen each other yesterday. He ran his hand over his head, and the familiar gesture warmed her heart. "You know I was pretty messed up when I left."

"You mean with your drinking?"

He nodded. "You know I had a big problem with that. It was the only way I had to deal with Julie's death and my parents' decision not to accept her into the family."

"Have you stayed sober since you've been gone?"

"I haven't had a drink since that day I told you I'd stopped. But it's been a real struggle."

"Has it been more of a struggle since your father passed?"

"Yes. My father's death hit the family hard. It was so much to handle all at one time. My sister helped me out a lot with strengthening my faith."

"How are Trish's children? I'm assuming you spent a lot of time with them while you were in Chicago."

"Mark and Regina are fine. Trish and I are thankful that Mark hasn't gotten into any more trouble, but we still think he feels hurt because his father won't come to visit him very often."

"Did you find a church home in Chicago?"

"Yes. Although I have a church family in Chicago, I call Devon Crandall a lot since we've become friends. I also kept thinking about what you told me right before I returned to Chicago. You told me that I didn't need to fix myself before coming to Jesus, that He'd accept me as I am. I thought about that a lot over the last few months."

"I'm glad I said something that could help you. But did your father's death make you want to start drinking again?"

He stared at her with his beautiful brown eyes. "I was tempted to drink, yes. But I didn't. I had to pray to the Lord every day to make it through the day without having a drink." He opened his mouth as if he were going to say more, but he remained silent.

"Were you going to say something else?"

"No." Silence filled the kitchen, almost as if

each of them had to digest the presence of the other.

Frank massaged her fingers, and she didn't have the strength to pull away. "I've missed you so much. You don't know how many times I've picked up the phone to call you but then decided against it."

She shrugged as feelings of joy and apprehension continued to course through her veins. "Why didn't you call? I wondered how you were doing. I sent you a Christmas card, and you never responded."

He sighed. "Because I had so many things to sort through and to work out in my life, I didn't want to call you before I'd set my life straight," he repeated.

"So, everything is fine with you now?"

"Yes, it is. I asked if I could transfer back to the Dairy office, and they let me transfer."

"And now what are you going to do?"

"I'd like for us to date and get to know each other again."

Emily couldn't believe it. "Date me?"

He sat up. "I'm a new man now. I'd like for you to get to know me better, and I'd like to spend some time with you again."

"I can't believe you did all this—relocated and everything—without calling me first. You could have warned me you were coming."

"I was sitting on the porch when you were

talking to Cameron. I heard everything he said. I know you don't have feelings for him."

Emily inwardly winced. It was awful that Frank had heard such a private conversation. It was also highly upsetting that Cameron had mentioned Frank when they were talking. Before she could speak, Frank made another comment. "Are you dating somebody else besides Cameron?"

"I don't think that's any of your business." He dropped her hand, frowning. "I'm sorry. I shouldn't have said that."

"You're angry with me."

"I'm just. . .I'm just surprised to see you. You didn't even call me to tell me you were coming. You could have at least called and let me know you'd be here instead of sneaking on my porch and waiting for me."

He frowned. "I wasn't sneaking. It's not my fault that you were out on a date when I decided to come."

"You could have at least warned me that you'd be here."

"I felt the Lord leading me to come back here and live. I should have called you, but I guess I just wasn't thinking clearly. I wanted to surprise you."

"Well, you did surprise me. I—"

"I love you." His voice was so low that she had to strain to hear it.

"What?"

"I said I love you, Emily. I know it's hard to

believe, but I do. I've loved you for months, but I knew there was no hope between us until I straightened out my life." He scooted closer to her and kissed her palm.

She pulled her hand away. "I don't know if I'm ready for us to date, Frank."

His mouth drooped. "I understand. Will you at least think about going out with me tomorrow?" When she remained silent, he found pen and paper on the kitchen counter. After writing something down, he placed the paper in her palm. "I've missed you, Emily, and I hope you'll let me take you out tomorrow. Here's my new phone number. Just call me and let me know when you've decided if you'd like to spend some time together."

She mutely nodded, still trying to come to terms with his sudden presence in her home. "Remember that I do love you, Emily. Just give me some time to show you how I feel and how I've changed. I'll try not to disappoint you." He stated the words as if he were making a vow.

Emily nodded, watching him leave, already deciding she would go out with him the following day.

CHAPTER 17

FRANK WHISTLED AS he prepared for his date with Emily the next day. *Lord, please help Emily to forgive me and accept me into her live again. Amen.* He had purchased a large heart-shaped box of imported Swiss chocolates and an exquisite diamond pendant.

He ran his fingers over the sparkling gem, imagining the jewel nestled against Emily's caramel-colored throat. He then grabbed his coat, headed out the door, and drove down the familiar route to the Coopers' farm.

Since he was now renting an apartment near Dairy, he arrived at Emily's house in minutes and knocked at her door. He heard the sound of high heels clicking on the kitchen floor before Emily opened the door.

His eyes widened when he saw her wearing a fancy burgundy dress with matching shoes. Her short hair framed her face, drawing attention to her full copper-colored lips and the tiny freckles sprinkled across her nose.

He kissed her hand. "Emily, it's good to see you again."

She nodded, leading him into the living room. "I'm glad to see you, too."

He glanced around the silent house. "Where's your stepmom?" They sat on the tattered couch as he placed his bag of gifts on the scarred wooden coffee table.

"She's upstairs taking a nap."

"Is she okay?"

"She's fine. After work yesterday and today she was with a family in need with the church outreach. She just came home a few hours ago, so she said she wanted to take a nap." Emily frowned as she glanced up the stairs.

"What's wrong?"

She shrugged. "Laura's been different since her daughter had the baby."

"How?"

She shrugged again. "It's hard to say. I know something has been bothering her for a long time, but she won't talk to me about it."

"Maybe you should ask her about it again. I'm sure if it was something important she would have told you by now."

"No. Don't assume that. Laura can be close-mouthed about a problem for a long time before she says anything about it."

"I'm sure Laura will tell you when she's ready." He paused for a few seconds, glancing around the room. "So, how have you been?"

"Okay, I guess."

"Do Jeremy and Darren still come to help you milk the cows?"

"No, since basketball season started, they said it was too much for them to handle with classes and homework and all. They're both on the basketball team, so that complicates things with their schedules."

"So you're doing the milking by yourself every day?"

"Pretty much. I'll probably get somebody to help me when the weather turns warm again. I think I told you last summer that we go through five hay cuttings, so that's one thing that adds a lot of work during the summer months."

The floral scent of her perfume filled the room with sweetness. He took a deep breath, removing the chocolates and the pendant from the bag. He presented her with his gifts. "I bought these for you. I hope you like them."

She smiled, opening the small box and admiring the diamond pendant. "My goodness! You shouldn't be buying this for me." Her large eyes were full of apprehension as he removed the pendant and placed it on her neck. The gem twinkled against her caramel skin, and Frank was pleased with his purchase.

"I also brought you some candy."

"You really shouldn't be buying this for me. I haven't seen you for months and—"

He squeezed her shoulder. "But it looks good on

you. If you don't want to wear it, I'll understand." He sighed with relief when she didn't attempt to remove the piece of jewelry. He checked his watch. "We'd better hurry if we want to get there before the comedy show begins."

She fingered the pendant before she stood. "Frank, I need to be honest with you. I still feel funny about your being here so suddenly."

"Emily, I know this is sudden. I probably should have handled this differently and called you first. How about we have a long talk about everything after the show?" When Emily nodded in agreement, they drove to Baltimore to see a Christian comedienne. Frank recalled Emily saying last summer how much she'd wanted to see this entertainer when she came to town, so he was glad he had been able to secure tickets. He tried to enjoy the funny skits during the show, but the sad, despondent look in Emily's eyes haunted him throughout the evening.

Afterward they stopped for hot chocolate at Starbucks. She still seemed sad, so he took her hand, wanting to make her feel better.

She finally smiled, pulling her hand away before sipping her hot drink. She looked outside at the people passing by the window.

"What's on your mind, Emily?"

"I was just thinking that because of you, I'm still living on my farm. Due to the increase of robberies in town, my stepmother insisted we get an alarm system, and we could afford it since you had. . .helped us out financially like that." She squeezed his hand. "Frank, I am truly grateful for what you did for me and Laura. I really am. I've already made a few payments to you and I promise we'll pay the rest of the money back," she said softly, her eyes suddenly filling with tears.

His heart skipped a beat when he moved to her side of the table and sat beside her, pulling her into his arms.

"Emily, I'm not worried about the money. Now, what's the matter?"

He relished the feel of her soft hair in the crook of his neck, her tears splattering against his crisp white shirt. "Oh, it's nothing." Her slim brown body fit into his arms perfectly. He just wanted to hold her forever.

"Well, something must be wrong if you're crying." He never would understand why women were so strange.

She sniffed. "My life has just been so crazy since my daddy passed. I had to get used to his death; then you showed up, and then I had to get used to the attraction we shared while I came to grips with the fact that you were an unsaved alcoholic. Then you found that incriminating evidence against my father, and I had to get used to the fact that my father wasn't as perfect as I thought him to be." She swallowed as he continued to hold her. Her hands were shaking, so he took her hands into his, hoping to calm her down. "Then I wondered if there were other facts about my father that I needed to know about." She gave him a watery smile, and he handed her a tissue. She blew her nose and gazed out the window.

"Go on," he urged.

She sniffed loudly. "Then you helped me save my farm, and then you left." She snapped her fingers to emphasize her point. "Even though you said good- bye, I still wondered if you were coming back. And then, months later, you appear on my doorstep to pick up where we left off like nothing was wrong. Yes, things have been a bit crazy since the beginning of last summer, Frank. I feel like my life has been one big emotional roller coaster."

He released her and faced her directly. Her head was down, so he lifted her chin with his fingers, staring directly into her watery eyes. "I hurt you when I left suddenly?" The realization of what he did hit him like a freight train. She nodded. "I'm so sorry, Emily. I was thinking about turning my life around, getting myself back together in Chicago. Leaving seemed to be the best choice." He blew air through his lips, still gazing at her. "Plus, I knew I was in love with you, and I couldn't stand being around you all the time, seeing you, knowing we couldn't be together because I was an alcoholic. I guess I was too selfish to realize how my actions might hurt you."

He pressed his lips to her forehead. "You know, staying wasn't an option for me. When my dad died, you don't know how close I came to drinking again." He took her hand. "I'm still struggling with my alcoholism, and I wanted to be sure that I'd been sober for a long time before I came back here. I wanted to be here with you. I wanted to see you, but I felt like if I were here and started drinking again, things wouldn't have worked out with us, and I would have hurt you more by being here instead of staying away." He squeezed her fingers. "Please say you'll forgive me. I do love you, and I hope that you'll believe me eventually."

"I understand why you left, but I still have a hard time starting over with you again." She grabbed a napkin and wiped her eyes. "You know, I was wondering why you bought me those gifts."

He frowned. "What do you mean?"

She touched the pendant. "You leave for six months, and then you show up at my house with this necklace, thinking that things are fine between us and we can start dating."

He shrugged again. "So?"

"So, it almost seems like you're trying to bribe me to go out with you. I feel like you want to use your money to buy nice things to fix the situation so that you can get your way."

"What else am I supposed to do?" He threw his hands up in the air, exasperated.

"Frank, this necklace means nothing to me. It's pretty and I love it, but if I could exchange this necklace for some of your time during your six-month absence so that I wouldn't have had to worry about you so much, I'd exchange it in a heartbeat."

He gripped his cup. "Do you mean to tell me that you would exchange the necklace just so you could have had some contact with me when I disappeared for six months?"

She nodded. "If you had just kept me in the loop and talked to me and told me that you might possibly return, my mind would have been more at ease, and I would have felt better." She continued to caress the necklace. "This necklace is just a piece of jewelry, but your honesty is priceless. Do you understand?"

"I think so. I'm sorry. It's just that. . ."

Emily touched his wrist, urging him to continue. "Go on."

"It's just that, growing up, my father wasn't always nice to my mother. He had affairs, and my mother would get upset and cry. He always managed to buy her something—expensive jewelry or a trinket that she would like. Things would be better for a few months before he started acting up again." He sipped his chocolate. "I thought women liked getting nice things, and I thought it showed how much I want to spend time with you."

He looked out the window, staring at the people walking down the side- walk. "You know how I take a special interest in Trish's children and how I used to mentor boys at the rec center in Chicago?"

"Yes."

"Well, while I was home, I thought about why I'm so passionate about kids having a father in their lives, especially boys. As I've been meeting with alcoholic support groups, talking things out, I've discovered that my passion for that stems from the way I wished my dad had treated me. He always provided for Trish and me financially, but we didn't do a whole lot of things together as a family. He was gone a lot, working long hours, and he was always going away on business trips."

"Frank, you've never told me any of this before."

"Honey, I don't think I even realized half this stuff about myself until recently."

"It sounds like your time away has given you a chance to really think about your life."

He agreed before taking another sip of his hot drink. "Anyway, Julie, when I was married to her, used to complain about my buying her things after we'd had an argument. She said my generosity didn't make the problem go away and that we needed to talk about it."

She nodded. "Julie was right. But you're just following your father's example, so it's understandable why you would think that a new item might make a woman feel better." She changed the subject. "Were you able to straighten out your relationship with your parents?"

"I'm glad I went to Chicago, because both Trish and I were able to spend some quality time with my father before he passed. We convinced him to accept Christ before his death."

Emily squeezed his hand. "That's wonderful, Frank."

He nodded. "Things are still a little shaky with my mom. In my heart, I feel I've forgiven them for the way they treated Julie, but I still feel bad for my mom. She's still not saved, but Trish and I are working on her. She's grieving so hard for my dad, and Trish and I are doing all that we can to console her."

"At least Trish is still there in Chicago with her. Did your mother object to your leaving again?"

Frank thought about his mother. "Yes, she objected a lot, but I felt strongly about coming back and seeing you again, and I didn't think it was right for me to stay away. She accused me of abandoning my familial duties since my dad had passed. I reminded her that Trish and her family were in Chicago to keep her company."

"Does she know about me?"

"Yes."

"Does she know that I'm a dairy farmer? I know she didn't approve of Julie's background. I'm not from a privileged background either."

He didn't want to tell her that his mother already objected to his dating her. Since he sensed Emily was already apprehensive about having a relationship with him, he certainly didn't want to scare her away with that fact. "Let's not talk about my mom right now. Let's talk about us."

She stared at the whipped cream and marshmallows floating on her cup of hot chocolate. "Frank, I'm not sure this is such a good idea."

His heart skipped a beat. "What do you mean?"

She pointed to the hot chocolate. "Us spending time together, drinking hot chocolate, dating, whatever you call it."

His mouth dropped open. He fingered the tiny mole on the side of her neck. "Emily, I've told you how much I've changed over the last six months. The least you can do is give me a chance to prove myself. Why would you not want us to date?"

She looked at him, her eyes sparkling with fear and apprehension. "I can't deny there is something between us, but even though you're saved now, I find it hard to trust you." She raised her hands in the air. "You've been gone for six months with hardly any contact. If we start dating and then I get emotionally involved with you, what's to stop you from leaving again for another six months?" She fingered the paper mug. "What if you leave again and never come back?"

"Oh, Emily." He tried to pull her into his arms, but she pushed him away. "Frank, you need to give me some time and space to think and pray about this. I feel so confused right now."

He closed his eyes briefly, silently praying for a

way to make her understand how much he truly loved her. "I'll be praying for you, too, Emily."

She raised her eyebrows. "You'll be praying for me?"

He nodded. "Yes. I'll be praying that God will make you understand just how much you mean to me. I'll also pray that God will soften your heart to forgive me for leaving you for six months." He stopped and swallowed, still trying to find the right words to say. "I'll also hope and pray that Jesus will allow you to trust me. I know you don't trust me right now, but maybe, just maybe, that'll change."

"It just sounds so odd, you speaking of prayer."

He shrugged. "I told you I've accepted Christ. I'm a saved man, so of course I'm going to pray."

She seemed to be thinking about his statement, weighing his words. "I do need some time to think about this." Her toffee-colored fingers caressed the sparkling diamond nestled on her neck. "I also think you should take your gift back. It's not right for me to accept such an expensive item from you if I'm not sure what's going to happen between us."

"Keep the necklace."

"But, Frank, I really don't feel comfortable accepting things from you."

He sighed. "Why don't you keep the gifts until you decide what you'd like to do? Think and pray about it for as long as you want. Take all the time you need. I understand why you're hesitant about spending time with me again. When you feel more comfortable about it, just let me know, and we can talk about it."

They were silent as the whirring sound of the espresso machine filled the shop. Frank finally spoke. "Come on, I'll take you home now."

She nodded, then stood and gathered her coat. "All right." She remained silent as he helped her put on her coat, and they walked to his car.

CHAPTER 18

THE FOLLOWING SUNDAY, Emily stood in the pew, accompanying the choir with the rest of the congregation in the closing hymn. Laura grabbed her arm after they exited the sanctuary. Before Laura could speak, Kelly walked toward them from the front of the church, still sporting her red-and -white choir robe. "Emily, I've been meaning to call you for the last few days, but I've been busy." She seemed slightly out of breath, and tendrils of dark hair fell into her face.

Laura squeezed Emily's arm. "Kelly, did you know Frank was back in town? I just saw him in the sanctuary."

Kelly frowned, staring at the older woman. "Of course I did, Mrs. Cooper. Didn't you know?"

"No, I didn't." She gazed at her stepdaughter. "Now I understand why you've been so quiet and moody the last couple of days. Why didn't you tell me that Frank was back? Have you had a chance to speak with him yet?"

Frank entered the foyer. "Yes, Laura, I've seen your daughter. Twice."

Emily glanced at Frank. "Hi, Frank."

He smiled, touching her shoulder. "Hi, Emily."

Laura focused on Frank. "You've changed so much over the last six months, Frank, I barely recognized you sitting in front of the sanctuary. How are you?" She embraced him, and he smiled.

"I've been okay. A lot has been going on in my life since I've been gone."

Laura's brown eyes twinkled. "Well, we're going out to lunch. Why don't you join us and tell us all about it?"

He looked at Emily briefly before focusing on Laura again. "I'm afraid I can't, but you ladies have yourselves a nice lunch." He waved, following the rest of the crowd out of the church.

"Emily Jane Cooper, what in the world is going on here?" Her stepmother folded her arms in front of her chest, impatiently tapping her foot. Kelly stared at Emily also, and Emily felt as if she were being judged by a jury.

"Emily." Kelly grabbed her arm, and Emily gazed at her best friend.

"What?"

"Let me put my choir robe away. Then we can go to lunch, and you can tell me and your mom what's happening between you and Frank."

Okay."

"Hi, Emily." Christine approached in a fetching purple dress.

"Hey Christine." Emily hugged her friend.

Emily's stepmother fingered Christine's dress. "That's a pretty dress, Christine. We're about to go to lunch if you'd like to join us."

Soon they were seated amid the Sunday afternoon crowd at the local diner. Emily told her mother, Kelly, and Christine about the two times she'd seen Frank and about her fears. "I've been praying about it, and I want to date Frank, I really do, but it's just so hard to trust him after all that's happened. Also, I'm wondering what will happen when he has rough times. Will he still turn to alcohol? I know he's saved, but that doesn't mean he's perfect."

"Neither are you," Kelly retorted.

Emily glared at Kelly. "What's that supposed to mean?"

"Frank explained why he left. He told you himself how messed up his life was before he found Christ. He finally admitted he had a problem with alcohol, he beat his habit, he's accepted Christ, and now he's back. It may have taken him some time to be honest with you, but I can understand why he stayed away."

"But he could have said something before now. He only e-mailed and texted me a few times, and that was it."

Laura touched Emily's hand. "Honey, Kelly is right. I'm not saying you need to pick up where you left off, because you're right to be cautious, but maybe you can get to know each other again."

Emily shook her head. "I don't know."

Laura continued to speak. "Emily, I think Frank's silence was just his way of protecting you. He feared he wasn't strong enough to stay away from alcohol. He didn't want you to get emotionally involved with him if he ended up drinking again."

Kelly nodded. "I agree, Mrs. Cooper. I think it's good that you were honest with Frank, Emily. He knows he's made a mistake, and I'm sure he feels bad about hurting you. But I also sense that he felt as if he had no choice, because if he was here and he messed up again, he would have ended up hurting you even more."

Christine nodded. "I agree with Mrs. Cooper and Kelly. You need to date Frank and just take it slow. Get to know each other again. He's already told you that he loves you and wants to give you two a chance." She twirled the pearls around her neck. "You know, if you don't at least give him a chance, I think you'll regret it."

She glanced at her friend. "Do you think so?"

Christine nodded firmly. "Yes, I do think so. I could see you wondering for years and years what would have happened if you'd given Franklin Reese a chance way back when."

Emily ate the rest of her meal in silence, allowing Kelly, Christine, and her stepmother to chat without her input. At one point, Laura pulled out her wallet and showed Kelly and Christine recent pictures of her grandbaby.

Emily's mind was still plagued with thoughts about Frank when she milked the cows later that evening.

The following Sunday, Emily entered the sanctuary with her stepmother. She anxiously scanned the crowd of parishioners sitting in the wooden pews.

"Looking for somebody in particular?" Laura whispered in her ear.

Emily gritted her teeth, wishing her affection for Frank wasn't so obvious. She wondered where he was. The service was about to start, and he still had not shown up.

The choir entered the choir loft, and the small church was suddenly filled with holy music.

Kelly joyfully sang the opening hymn with the rest of the choir. Emily attempted to sway to the music, but thoughts of Frank and his whereabouts filled her mind.

When the choir completed their selections, Pastor Brown stepped into the pulpit, and his deep, booming voice filled the sanctuary. "Before I start the sermon this morning, I wanted to introduce one of our new members. I assume a lot of you have met Franklin Reese."

Emily's heart skipped a beat as she clutched her Bible. A few of the parishioners nodded in response.

"Well, he's been through a life-changing experience, and he's requested that I allow him to tell you all about it. So, here's Franklin Reese." He raised his hand toward the pulpit door, and Frank stepped onto the dais. They shared a handshake before Frank stood in front of the microphone.

Emily openly stared at the man who was slowly capturing her heart. He looked handsome sporting a dark suit and a cream-colored shirt and tie.

"Good morning."

"Good morning." Parishioners loudly responded to Frank's greeting.

"I've come to tell you this morning about how I came to accept Christ into my life."

During the next fifteen minutes, Emily listened to Frank tell details of his troubled college years and about the first time he realized he was an alcoholic. He then spoke of his sobriety, his first marriage, his strong love for his wife, her salvation, and her sudden violent death. "Friends, when my wife died, I felt a part of me had died also. I was mad, angry, and bitter. I was upset with my parents since they didn't accept my wife because of her background." He told of his return to alcoholism, the joy and warmth he received when attending Dairy Christian Church, and his support from Devon Crandall and the alcoholic support group. He mentioned there was a certain parishioner who urged him to accept Christ, and without mentioning a name, Frank's eyes met Emily's. He told of his salvation at Cylburn Arboretum and his sudden flee back to his hometown, hoping to put his life back in order.

He ended his testimony by telling how Christ had made a difference in his life. "My life is far from perfect, and I still have problems, but they don't seem like such a burden now that I'm relying on Jesus." A tear glistened on Frank's cheek as he spoke of the deep love he had for his Savior. The congregation stood, applauding Frank's courage in openly proclaiming his salvation journey.

Emily barely heard Pastor Brown's message afterward because she was still thinking about Frank's speech.

CHAPTER 19

A FEW WEEKS FOLLOWING Frank's testimony, Emily walked toward her house after milking the cows. She removed her barn boots before opening the door and entering her home. The scent of chicken filled the air as Laura removed a pan of biscuits from the oven. "Hi, Emily."

Emily sniffed. "Hi, Mom. You made chicken and dumplings and biscuits?" Her stomach grumbled with hunger. Smelled like this was going to be an awesome meal. What an unexpected treat after a long, exhausting day.

Laura smiled, but her eyes seemed sad as she looked at Emily. "Yes, I haven't made it in a long time, and I know how much you like my chicken and dumplings." Once Emily had washed up and changed, she joined her stepmother at the table. After Laura said grace, Emily piled her plate with food. "I made chocolate cake for dessert." Emily smiled before she said grace and then stuffed a bite of food into her mouth.

Laura tapped her foot, sipping a cup of coffee as Emily savored the tasty meal. "Aren't you going to eat?"

Laura shook her head. "I'm too nervous to eat."

Emily stopped eating, dropping her fork on her plate. "Why would you be nervous?"

Her stepmother's hand shook as she set her cup back on the saucer. "You've probably guessed that something heavy has been on my mind since Becky had her baby."

"Yes. When Frank came back to town, that was one of the first things I told him. I knew something was bothering you, but I didn't know what it was."

Laura sipped her coffee. "Well, you know how I've always wanted to improve my relationship with my daughters."

Emily nodded.

Laura shrugged. "I missed a lot of their childhoods because my ex-husband was granted custody. Although I saw them for a few weeks each summer, I still felt as if they resented me, especially Becky. She was only five when the divorce happened, and I sometimes think she blames me for what happened to her."

"Children are not always rational."

Laura shrugged again. "Adults are not always rational either." She stared at her coffee cup. "I think Becky still blames me a little bit for the divorce, but we've been discussing what's happened over the years, and I think we're getting closer. When Becky had her baby and we spent a lot of time together, she told me that she and her husband had discussed it, and eventually she wants to go back to work. She said she was tired of being a housewife and mother full-time and she wanted to reenter the workforce."

"But Becky has three kids now, and all of them are under five. Won't she and her husband be paying a lot in daycare costs if she decides to work again full-time?"

Laura took Emily's hand, looking directly into her eyes. "They won't have to pay as much in daycare costs if I'm taking care of their kids."

Her breath caught. "You're leaving?" The words squeaked from her lips like rusty hinges. Just saying that Laura was leaving left a deep emptiness inside of her. She loved her mom and she really wanted her to stay on the farm.

Laura nodded, squeezing Emily's hand. "Honey, I know when I first married your father, you and I got off to a rocky start, but I've grown to love you as a daughter."

"I love you, too, Mom."

"I've told you how I've always regretted not having a better relationship with my daughters. This is something that I really want to do. I can be there to help raise my grandchildren and solidify my relationship with Becky."

Emily wiped the tears from her eyes. "I'm going to be on this farm all by myself." She did not find the thought to be soothing. She recalled how empty the house felt when Laura was gone the other two times.

"Honey, I know. I've been struggling with this decision since I returned last September. That's what's been bothering me so much. I never said anything, because Becky didn't have a job yet."

Emily sniffed as Laura handed her a tissue. As she dried her eyes, she noticed that Laura was crying also. "So, Becky's found a job?"

"Yes. She's going to be starting in one month, so I'm not leaving right away, but I promised her I would be there to help out when it's time for her to start her new job. We've already spoken about the finances, and she'll be paying me an amount comparable to what I'd been earning in the lunch room at the school."

The shocking news rocked Emily's world, and the two women embraced before Emily finished her meal.

After Laura made her announcement about leaving, Emily spent the next few weeks thinking about her situation with Frank and praying about it. When Laura did leave, it was heartbreaking for Emily. She drove her stepmother to the airport and promised that if she found adequate help on the farm, she'd come and visit Laura and her family within the next year. She still participated in her church book club, and she was still involved in the singles ministry. She kept a busy routine, trying to figure out what to do about Frank. She didn't mention the matter anymore to Laura, Kelly, or Christine, but left it solely in the Lord's hands.

When Frank had been in town for a month and a half, Emily fell to her knees before bedtime, continuing to seek the Lord's guidance. "Lord," she whispered, "let me know what You want me to do. I keep thinking about Frank. When I see him at church, worshipping and praising You on Sunday, I just want to walk up the aisle, sit beside him, and praise You with him. I want to spend time with him and get to know him all over again now that he's a Christian. Does this mean he's the right man for me, Lord?" When she finished her prayer, calming peace flowed through her.

She slid between her crisp, clean cotton sheets, and when she awakened the next morning, she knew what she had to do.

CHAPTER 20

THE NEXT DAY was Saturday, and after Emily milked her cows and did some errands, she showered and changed into her favorite blue jeans and red shirt.

She had already discovered the location of Frank's new apartment from the gossip she'd heard through the church grapevine. She'd also heard that he volunteered every other Saturday at the rec center in a nearby town. She drove to his apartment building in Dairy, saying a silent prayer during the entire journey. She took a deep breath and knocked on his door, wondering if she should have called before traipsing to his apartment unannounced.

The rusty hinges creaked when the door swung open. "Emily!"

Emily clenched her hands together, staring at Frank. "Frank, I wanted to talk with you. I hope it's all right."

He smiled, stroking his beard. "Emily, you're always welcome in my home. Come in." She stepped into the living room, trying to ignore the clothes and newspapers scattered on the hardwood floor. A heavenly scent of tomatoes and spices spilled from the small kitchen. "What are you cooking?"

"Spaghetti and meatballs. I made some garlic bread, too."

Surprised, she glanced into the kitchen before looking at Frank again. A disturbing thought fluttered through her mind. "You made all this for lunch?"

"Yes."

"Are you expecting somebody?" Had she waited too long to give him an answer, and he'd already started dating? She noticed how the single women at church swarmed after Frank like bees to honey.

"No."

"Then why did you make all this for lunch?" He motioned toward the kitchen, not answering her question. "I'm getting ready to eat right now if you're interested." He caressed her with his dark brown eyes, and her heart thudded. When her tummy rumbled, he chuckled. "You still haven't changed. I see you still have a noisy stomach."

She chuckled, and he led her into the kitchen and pulled out a chair for her. She sat, and he served up plates of spaghetti and meatballs, salad, and garlic bread. "I've missed having home-cooked food since Laura's been gone."

Frank nodded. "I can understand that. Have you heard from her?"

"We call each other regularly. She sounds happy, and I think she's glad that she's growing closer to her daughter and her grandchildren." Frank took her hand and bowed his head. In his deep, strong voice, he thanked the Lord for their food. Emily said amen and squeezed his hand. She took a bite of the food and moaned. "Oh my…"

"What's the matter?"

She licked her lips, taking another bite of spaghetti before sampling the crunchy garlic bread. "This is the best spaghetti I've *ever* had." She sampled more food. "Mmm. This garlic bread is excellent."

He laughed, watching her eat. "I'm glad you like it so much."

"I can't believe you made all this yourself."

"I don't use spaghetti sauce out of a jar. I make my own, and I made the garlic bread myself, too."

"You cook?" She looked at him, and she felt as if she was seeing a new Frank, a different Frank from the way he was eight months ago.

"Yes, I cook."

"But when I went to your old apartment, you had pizza boxes and empty take-out containers all over the room. I thought you didn't know how to cook." They ate in silence, enjoying their meal. When they were finished, they took their lemonade into the living room, and Frank invited her to sit.

"I'm glad you came by. I wanted to talk to you about something."

She sat on the expensive leather couch. "Good, I wanted to talk to you, too."

"You were asking about my cooking earlier?"

"Yes."

"Well, cooking is something I used to do all the time before Julie died. When she died, I started drinking, and I just stopped doing the things I loved, like cooking." He sipped his lemonade. "I was so bitter and angry that the only thing that brought me pleasure was alcohol. You know when I left you for six months and my dad died?" She nodded. "Well, I was a real mess back then."

"I know, you told me that."

"No, I didn't tell you how bad of a mess I was. When my dad died, I was so afraid that I was going to start drinking again that I took a month-long leave of absence from work." He squeezed her hand. "I'd initially wanted a partnership at the accounting firm. All of that changed. I wasn't partnership material…well.. after everything that happened. I'd wanted it to earn more money from the partnership so that…so that I could help financially assist youth groups in community centers."

"Frank, that's noble of you. You still might get your partnership someday."

"Maybe." He sighed. "You know, Emily, even though I was saved, the urge to drink consumed me so much that I went to a medical doctor, and he had to give me medicine to help with my cravings."

She touched his arm. "Are you still on the medicine?"

"No, I stopped taking it a few months before I decided to come back here. But I was off work for a whole month, helping my mother out and just straightening out my life. There's an alcoholic support group that meets each day in Chicago. It's not always the same people, but I made sure I was there every day. Being with the other members helped me stay sober. I read my Bible like crazy. I was drinking in the Word, and I had so many questions about the scriptures. My church in Chicago was awesome, and they answered all my questions about God and the Bible. I found that I had a lot of learning to do." He pointed toward his Bible. "I don't think I could've made it through this whole ordeal if it weren't for God."

He paused for a moment, then said softly, "You know, Emily, I love reading the scriptures. There's so much wisdom between those pages." He looked toward the window for a minute, as if thinking of what he should say. "Anyway, during my absence, I learned that I not only had to continue placing my faith in God, but I also had to get into the things that brought me pleasure."

"Like cooking?"

He squeezed her hand. "Yes, like cooking. It's something to do to keep my mind off drinking."

"Do you still have the urge to drink?"

He looked at her. "Honey, the urge to drink never goes away; you just have to learn to be strong and not act on it. It's scary thinking about not ever having another drink, but you have to take it one day at a time."

She blew air through her lips. "I didn't realize that."

"I had to let you know all this. I'd still like us to get to know each other again. I'm different now."

"That's what I wanted to talk to you about."

"Oh?"

"Yes. I think I'd like to give us a chance. I wondered if we could get to know each other as friends again."

His lips touched her nose. "I'm too attracted to you to be just your friend, but I'd like to spend time with you again."

She smiled at him. "I'm attracted to you, too. And I have an admission of my own to make."

He chuckled. "What's that?"

"I'm a lousy cook."

He laughed. "I know. You told me that when I first met you. Maybe my cooking skills will balance everything out between us."

She smiled. "Yes, maybe your cooking skills will balance everything out."

He then leaned toward her and kissed her. So, sweet, just as she'd remembered. As he pulled her into his arms, she sighed. His kisses were as smooth and sweet as the syrup she'd used on her pancakes that morning.

During the next few months, Frank continued to struggle with his decision to ask Emily to marry him. Even though they were getting to know each other better, he still faltered with his alcoholism. It was a daily struggle, and he prayed each day for the strength to let go and trust himself and believe in the Lord enough to trust his decision to marry Emily.

As he got to know Emily again, he found his love for her grew as the days passed. Since Laura was gone, Emily was out at the farm alone, and he often worried about her living by herself in the country, running the farm solo. He visited often after work, and he realized she wasn't kidding when she said she couldn't cook. His frequent late-evening visits often included takeout. Sometimes in the evenings, while she was in the barn milking the cows, he'd stop at the grocery store to buy food to make dinner for her.

He knew he had really fallen hard for her when he arrived unexpectedly at five in the morning on a Saturday. He'd worn his oldest clothing and a pair of battered sneakers. After parking in the driveway, he traipsed to the familiar barn. The cows were chained in their stalls, eating their piles of food. He recalled Emily telling him about the corn, soybeans, and alfalfa they grew to make feed for the cows. A clear liquid squished through the pipes, and Frank found Emily in the room where the milk tank and sink were located. "Frank." Her eyes shone with delight as they embraced. "What are you doing here?"

"I know you like having somebody to help you milk the cows, so I came to give you a hand." Since Emily had been milking the cows most of her life, he figured he'd be more of a hindrance than a help. But he was determined to learn how to milk so he could help her eventually. He gestured toward the sink. "What are you doing?"

"I'm cleaning the pipes and the equipment with an acid and water solution before I start milking."

He washed his hands before he followed her as she went into the barn carrying the mobile milking units. She gave him a pair of gloves. "It's important that I clean the udders of each cow using an iodine dipper." She left and returned with a steaming bucket of liquid.

"I could have carried that in here for you."

She laughed. "Well, you can carry it next time if you make it to another milking."

If he made it to another milking? He was serious about this. They were partners in doing the milking – she just didn't realize it yet. Since he felt so uneasy cleaning the teats and udders of each cow and attaching the units, Emily ended up doing most of the milking herself. Nevertheless, it felt good to be out in the barn with her, watching her do the chores. He found that he was a better help once the cows were milked. She pushed a cart full of feed and handed him a shovel. "After milking we feed the cows grain, soybeans, and corn feed." She showed him what to do. "Just shovel some in front of each stall. After they're done, we need to let them out to graze a bit. I'm going to clean the milking equipment." As he shoveled feed, he glanced at the pipes, noting that clear liquid again swished through them as Emily did her cleanup. Once they'd cleaned the floor and let the cows out, he followed her to the porch. She removed her barn boots, and he took off his shoes, wiggling his toes.

"Thanks for helping me this morning, Frank." He shrugged.

"I'm not sure if I was much help."

She touched his arm. "You were a big help." He leaned toward her and kissed her forehead.

Once they'd washed up, Frank made bacon, eggs, and toast for breakfast. Once he said grace over their meal and they were eating, Emily told him something. "My sister, Sarah, called me last night."

"Did she want money?" Emily had once mentioned that her sister only called when she wanted something.

"Yes."

"How much did she want?"

"She said she needed two hundred dollars to pay her phone bill. If she doesn't pay it soon, they're going to turn her phone off."

"Are you going to give it to her?"

Emily shrugged. "I don't know. I told her I'd have to think and pray about it. I said I'd call her back in a couple of days to let her know what I'd decided to do." She sipped her juice. "Have you spoken to your mother lately?"

He sighed, spreading butter and jelly on his toast. "Yes."

"How is she doing?"

"She's doing okay." He didn't bother to mention that his mother had not been vocal about his dating life in a long time. He still wasn't sure if she was learning to accept his choices or if she had more pressing things on her mind. "Trish spends time with her every week, so I'm glad about that."

"How are the kids doing?"

"They're doing fine. Next month is Regina's birthday. I'm flying up to Chicago for that." He stopped eating and took her hand. "I'd like for you to come with me if you can get somebody to do the milking for you."

"I'd love to come with you, Frank, but I can't make any promises. I'll see if I can find somebody to do the chores for me the weekend of the party."

They continued to eat in silence for a few minutes. "I'm going to the rec center later today. You know, I didn't realize how much I missed spending time with young people until I started doing it again."

"Yeah, I can tell you enjoy it. It's nice of you

to spend time mentoring the kids at the center." After a few moments, she touched his arm. "I enjoyed having you with me this morning to milk the cows. It was nice."

He took her hand, squeezing her fingers. "I enjoyed doing it with you. Is it okay if I come and help you milk on the weekends?"

Emily returned his squeeze. "Yes, I'd like that very much."

Later that day, Frank found a store in Dairy that sold barn boots. When he returned to Emily's for the next milking, he brought his new footwear with him. He left his new barn boots at Emily's, placing them right beside hers.

CHAPTER 21

WHEN FRANK HAD been helping Emily milk cows for a couple of months, he finally felt it was time to ask her to marry him. On the day he purchased the ring from the jeweler, he called his mother. "Hello, Franklin." His mother was one of the few relatives who still called him by his full name.

He hesitated. "Mom, hi."

"You've got a worried tone in your voice, son."

"How are you?"

His mother spoke for five minutes about her health and how her regular visits with Trish and her grandchildren were going. Frank blurted his news before he lost his courage. "I'm going to ask Emily to marry me."

"Emily? That farmer you told me about when you came home?"

"Yes, Mom. You can't treat her the way you treated Julie. I don't like that kind of behavior." He failed to mention that his parents' actions had intensified his grief after Julie's violent death. "I love her too much to hurt her like that. She's a strong, proud woman, and she's running that farm by herself right now." When she remained silent, he mentally said a quick prayer before he reminded her how he'd met Emily through his job and how they'd grown closer in recent months. "If she says yes, then she'll be a part of the family."

"This is so sudden…"

Frank still wondered what was going through his mother's mind. "It's not so sudden. I just explained how long I've known her. I love her, Mom, and it'll hurt me if you reject her for superficial reasons." When his mother remained silent, he finally ended the call. Once he'd hung up the phone, he fell to his knees. "Lord, please, if this is your will and Emily says yes, please make everything work out with my mom. Amen."

When Emily arrived at Frank's apartment for their Saturday night dinner date, the sight of the lit tapered candles on the table made her stop and stare. "Why are we eating by candlelight?" She had been a bit suspicious when he'd called earlier, saying he would not be by that evening to help her with the milking.

He pulled her into his arms, kissing her nose. "I

just wanted to share a romantic dinner with you. What's wrong with that?"

She shook her head. "Nothing."

"I think you sometimes forget how much I enjoy your company." He led her to the table. "Let's eat."

When he placed the shrimp cocktail on the table, she looked at him. "Shrimp cocktail?"

He took her hand, asking the Lord to bless their food. Once they said their amens, he pointed at the food. "I made crab cakes and rice pilaf for dinner."

"All my favorites." When he continued to hold her hand, she wondered when they were going to dig into their meal. He kissed her fingers, and she closed her eyes, enjoying the feel of his lips against her skin.

"I have a question for you." His voice was low and husky, and his dark eyes shone in the candlelight.

He released her hand and pulled a small velvet box out of his pocket. He presented it to her. When she popped the box open, the diamond solitaire ring glittered. "Frank…"

"Will you marry me, Emily? You know how much I love you." "Yes, I'll marry you. I love you, Frank."

He pulled her into his arms, and they shared a blissful kiss.

EPILOGUE

FRANK STOOD AT the altar of Dairy Christian Church, his smile so wide he thought his face would split apart. Christine, Kelly, Trish, and Emily's sister, Sarah, served in the wedding as bridesmaids. Their canary yellow dresses looked becoming as the bright sunlight streamed through the church's stained-glass windows. Mark, decked out in his tuxedo, was a junior groomsman, and Regina served as a junior bridesmaid.

His mother sat in the front of the church, looking uncomfortable as she scanned the crowd. Both he and Trish were trying to convince their mother that her strict way of judging others was wrong, and so far she'd been cordial to Emily, not shunning her the way she'd shunned Julie.

Laura Cooper sat in the front row, crying openly. Since Frank was going to live with Emily on her dairy farm, Laura had confided to him that she felt better about her decision to leave and move in with her daughter.

Frank's heart palpitated when Emily walked

down the aisle. He'd booked their honeymoon to Tahiti as a surprise for Emily. He knew how much she craved seeing the gorgeous Tahitian beach and swimming with the sting rays.

He eyed her as she slowly walked down the aisle. She was the most beautiful woman he'd ever seen. Her white silky dress complemented her smooth brown skin. As Devon Crandall and his other friends from church served as ushers, Frank and Emily vowed to love each other forever.

The boat sped on the beautiful aquamarine water. Frank held her hand as he kissed her, long and deep. They'd rented a small private boat for the afternoon. Thankfully, their tour guide didn't pay them any attention as they kissed and hugged. Warmth surrounded them like a snuggly blanket at they stared at the beautiful mountains of Tahiti. "This is so beautiful." She just couldn't believe that she was here, in Tahiti, with Frank, on their honeymoon.

In the distance, two dolphins leapt into the air. "Amazing." Frank's deep voice filled with awe as he admired the sea creatures.

"You want a piece of candy?" Emily offered Frank a piece of the tasty vanilla hard candy made by the Tahitian natives. The tour guide had left an entire box for them to enjoy. So far, she'd eaten three pieces of the amazing sweet treat.

"Thanks." Frank unwrapped a piece of candy and popped it into his mouth. Once the boat stopped in the middle of the blue Pacific Ocean, they climbed out. The area where they'd temporarily stopped was shallow and as they stepped into the water, they sighed with pleasure. The cool, clear water felt good on this hot day.

They dropped breadcrumbs into the water and colorful fish swished through the water nipping at the meal. She giggled before looking directly into his eyes. "I love you Frank."

"I love you Emily." He pulled her into his arms and kissed her slowly, hungrily. She moaned and imagined the wonderful time they'd have when they returned to their bungalow later that evening.

THE END

If you enjoyed Milk Chocolate Kisses, then I'd really appreciate it if you left a sweet one or two-sentence review on one of these links: Amazon US or Amazon UK! Thank you! Reviews are often used by readers to find wonderful books.

EXCERPT

CHAPTER 1

KAREN EYED HERSELF in the mirror one last time. Simple, classy, elegant. She grinned. She looked fabulous in her cream-colored suit and high-heeled shoes. Ever since her date with her fiancé Lionel last week, the Sunday Founder's Day Service at her church had been on her mind. Over a romantic dinner, he'd hinted that he had some big news to share with her after the Founder's Day Service.

She giggled as she got patted her hair, which, she'd coiffed into a perfect French roll. Elegant curls dangled at the side of her head. Strolling as quickly as she could in her high heels, she locked the door to her apartment and got into her car. As she drove to church, she couldn't help smiling. She giggled as she stopped at a light. "Lord, thank you for this beautiful day. I feel so blessed. Amen." As she pulled away from the light, she gripped the steering wheel. *Lord, I'm so happy that I don't know what to do with myself.*

She'd not heard from Lionel over the last

couple of days. He'd been away at a finance conference and he'd said he'd be too busy to talk. He promised to make it up to her once he returned. He was supposed to land at five AM that morning. He was meeting her at church for the late service. After church, he was taking her out to lunch at Genevieve's, an elegant French restaurant. He only took her there for special occasions. The last time they'd dined there, it'd been when he'd proposed to her. She grinned as she pulled into the church parking lot. *Lord, Lionel is going to finally set a date for our wedding today.* He'd been hesitant about setting a date. They'd been engaged for months, and every time she'd broached setting a date, he always changed the subject. Well, she knew he wanted to get married. What man would purchase an engagement ring for a woman unless he were serious about marriage?

Before exiting the car, she scrutinized her left hand. The solitaire diamond ring sparkled under the bright sunlight. She'd sit and stare at her ring for hours sometimes. She polished it every night so that it always looked nice. Oh, the ring was so beautiful. The two-carat king looked glorious against her brown skin. Whenever she looked at it, she thought about the deep love she shared with her future husband.

Well, enough time staring at her ring. She shivered with happiness. After they set their wedding date today, she'd order the save-the-date cards and start choosing the stationary for their wedding invitations. She was thinking of cream-colored invitations etched with gold lettering as she got out of the car and strolled toward the church. She stopped walking when she spotted two of her church acquaintances conversing. "Good morning." The joy spilled from her voice like warm, fragrant water.

Both of the middle-aged women looked up at her and then looked away, as if they were hiding something. Their actions reminded her of how she'd acted whenever she'd gotten caught sneaking cookies from the cookie jar before dinner. Both women then glanced her way again. "H-Hello." Their mumbled greeting seemed forced as they blatantly ignored her and returned to their whispered conversation.

Well, that was strange. Looked like she'd been interrupting an intense private conversation. She shrugged as she pushed the church doors open. Mr. D., the usher standing in the foyer, handed her a program. "Morning, Karen." His dark eyes appeared sad. What was wrong with everybody this morning? Mr. D. was always smiling. Maybe something had happened.

"Mr. D. what's wrong?"

"Pastor has an important announcement this morning."

She gripped her program and touched his arm. "Did someone get hurt…or did somebody die?" Quick as she could, she mentally scrolled through the list of sick and shut-in parishioners. *Lord, please let everybody be okay.*

"No. Nothing like that." He then turned toward the next person who strolled into the foyer. Her bright mood darkened, just a little bit, as she strolled into the sanctuary. She'd taken so long primping that morning that she'd barely made it to church on time. Her and Lionel always sat together near the front. Whomever arrived first, would always save the other person a seat. She sighed. No empty seats in the front. Where was Lionel?

She scanned the small crowd. Where was he? Was it just her imagination, or were some of the parishioners giving her strange looks?

She finally took a seat near the back. Her elation from moments ago wilted like spoiled lettuce. Where was Lionel? She pulled out her phone and texted him. *Where are you? Was your flight delayed? Church is about to start.*

Pastor Smith approached the podium. Silence filled the church as he adjusted the microphone. "Before we begin praise and worship, we need to make an announcement." He took a deep breath. "We recently discovered that the church bank account is nearly empty."

She gulped and gripped her hands together. Lionel was the church treasurer. Well, maybe he'd....opened another account or something. Once he showed up to church that morning, she was sure he'd straighten everything out.

Lionel was a good, honest man. From what she'd always heard, he was the best treasurer that this megachurch had ever had. Her heart thudded as she glanced at her phone. Her text remained unanswered. Oh, where was he?

"We have to speak to our treasurer Lionel Green. So far, our calls have remained unanswered and he's not been at home."

But he was at a finance conference. Didn't he tell the church that he'd be away for a few days? She had to find him and let the church know that everything would be okay. Lionel wouldn't steal money and lie…would he?

She gulped again as she held her phone in a tight grip. The room seemed too warm. The person sitting beside her leaned toward her and patted her hand, as if to offer comfort. She glanced around the church.

Some people were staring at her.

A few of the women glared at her, as if *she* were responsible for the empty bank account. Heat, thick and heavy, swept through her soul. Sweat beaded her forehead and trickled down her face. *Oh, Lord Jesus, I have to get out of here.* She stood up on her shaky legs and tromped out of the pew and down the aisle. Quick as she could, she rushed to the bathroom. She marched to a stall, slammed it closed and locked it. She dropped onto the toilet seat, using it as a chair. She couldn't pray, couldn't even think. Pain shot through her head like bullets. She squeezed her eyes shut. Her shoulders shook as tears slid down her face. She shoved a wad of toilet paper against her eyes and mouth and silently sobbed.

Two weeks later...

Karen shoved the church doors open while swiping away the hot, wet tears streaming down her face. "Pastor Smith, I can't believe Lionel is still missing." Her voice echoed as she ran into the church.

The elderly reverend and his wife, Candace, hugged Karen, patting her back. After they released her, Candace stroked Karen's shoulder. "Honey, something has just come to our attention."

"What's that?"

"The way we announced Lionel's disappearance and the empty bank account at church two weeks ago. The pastor and I were under the mistaken impression that you'd already been informed. Tara later told us that she couldn't contact you. She'd tried to call you but didn't get an answer."

She sighed, frowning. "But, I didn't receive any phone calls."

"Honey, we just realized that nobody spoke to you directly about this before we announced it. Tara insisted that she called you and left messages. We were shocked when you showed up at church that morning. We were also surprised that you didn't know. It was unkind to deliver the news the way that we did."

Well it was a moot point now. All they needed to do was focus on finding Lionel and figure out what happened. Candace pointed down the hall. "The police detective is in the boardroom, waiting to talk to you. Are you sure you're up for this?"

Karen wiped her eyes again and took a deep breath. *Lord help me.* She squeezed her hands into fists and took another breath. She really needed to get ahold of herself. The traumatic events which had occurred over the past couple of weeks played through her mind like a nonstop movie. She winced and moaned. Her fiancé, Lionel Adams, had been fired as church treasurer after being accused of stealing thousands of dollars from their megachurch. And it was rumored that the assistant treasurer, Michelle James, had aided him with the theft.

Like the rest of the congregation, Karen had been shocked when the allegations against Lionel were initially announced at church.

Karen turned toward Candace. She covered her trembling lips with her hand. "I'll— I'll do the best I can to—to answer his questions."

The threesome slowly exited the sanctuary and walked down the hallway, toward the boardroom. A moment later, the pastor stopped outside a closed door, placing his hand on Karen's shoulder. "Karen, Michelle is missing also."

Karen gasped, stepping away from the pastor. "That. . .that can't be true." She'd refused to believe the rumor that Michelle had aided Lionel with the alleged theft.

He nodded. "Unfortunately, it is." He took a deep breath. "The church leadership team is concerned for both her and Lionel's welfare. We want to find them, but we can't ignore what's happened."

Candace took her hand. "Honey, we have to do all we can to locate them. What if there was foul play involved? Don't you want to make sure Lionel is safe?" More tears rushed from Karen's eyes, and she wiped the moisture away. Her head pounded as she leaned against the cool wall. She really needed to calm down. She focused on the coolness of the tiled wall against her hot skin.

Pastor Smith touched her shoulder. "Are you okay?"

Pulling herself away from the wall, she sighed. *God, give me strength.* "I–I'm okay now."

The pastor gestured toward the door. "The detective is in here. We called you to be questioned first since you know Lionel so well."

Karen glanced at Candace. "Nobody told the congregation exactly how much money Lionel may have stolen. We just know it was thousands of dollars. How much cash was missing?"

The woman released Karen's hand and looked at her husband, frowning. The pastor paused before speaking. "Fifty thousand dollars."

The room swayed as Karen leaned against the wall. Her head started spinning, as if a vicious cyclone spun in her brain. She whimpered and turned away. "Lord, please help me deal with this pain."

Candace patted her shoulder. "We'll take this one day at a time. The Lord will see us through."

Karen glanced at the closed door. How in the world would she find the courage to go in there? She rubbed her hands together. A few minutes alone, that's what she needed. After she took some time to settle down, pray a little bit, then she'd have the courage to do what she needed to do. "Is it okay if I go to the restroom before talking to the detective?"

Candace nodded. "Of course."

Leaving the couple, Karen walked to the bathroom, pushed the door open, and entered the room, desperately seeking a private moment with the Lord. Her heart skipped a beat when Tara Baker, the church secretary, dressed in an immaculate cream-colored suit and sporting stylish hair and polished fingernails, stepped out of the stall. Spotting Karen, her dark eyes widened.

While the secretary wordlessly washed her hands, Karen regarded her own worn jeans and faded T-shirt before touching her hair, which she'd pulled into a ponytail in her haste to get to the church. Maybe she should've taken time to change and freshen up before coming to the church.

"I always thought Lionel and Michelle were up to no good." Tara mumbled, drying her hands with a paper towel while glaring at Karen.

Could this day get any worse? Karen gritted her teeth. How in the world could Tara be so rude? As a Christian, she should've been offering her warmth, support, prayer…not cold rudeness. She opened her mouth, about to give this woman a piece of her mind, but Tara narrowed her eyes and leaned toward her.

"I find it hard to believe that you had no clue what your fiancé was doing behind your back." She was about confirm if Tara had tried to reach her when Lionel went missing. Before Karen could speak, Tara turned on her heels and strode out of the restroom.

Waves of pain floated through Karen's head as she struggled to blot out the secretary's unkind words. She squeezed her eyes shut and bowed her head. She needed to focus on Jesus right now. "God, please help me. Help us to find Lionel and Michelle. And keep them safe. Amen." Somewhat soothed, she rejoined the pastor and his wife.

Pastor Smith gestured toward the now–open door. "Karen, I'm so sorry about this."

Karen forced herself to smile before entering the room, silently praying for strength. The detective sat in a chair near the front of the room.

The minister gestured toward Karen. "Detective Ramsey, this is Karen Brown."

"Good morning, Karen." The dark-skinned, bald detective nodded toward her.

"Good morning," Karen mumbled, taking a seat near the detective. She turned to her minister. "Can you stay here with me, Pastor Smith?"

The clergyman touched her arm, gazing at the detective. "Is that okay with you, detective?"

Ramsey shrugged, opening his notebook. "If she wants you to stay, that's fine."

Pastor Smith settled into the empty chair beside her.

The investigator asked his first question. "Do you know where Lionel is?" "I. . ." She paused, chewing on her lower lip. "Before the church announced that he was fired, he told me he was going to go out of town for a conference and he said he'd visit his cousin for a few days afterwards. I haven't talked to him since, and th–that was over two weeks ago." She paused, gripping the arms of the chair. "I—I haven't been able to contact him since he left." She took a deep breath. "He won't answer his cell phone. I figured he wanted some time alone and I would see him when he returned for his hearing."

The detective looked up from the notes he was writing. "Where does his cousin live?"

As Ramsey's questions went on and on, Karen felt overwhelmed with worry, fatigue, and nausea.

Hot tears flowing down her cheeks, she prayed, *Lord, will I ever feel normal again?*

Her head pounded with pain, and she began rubbing her temples. Pastor Smith touched her elbow. "Are you all right?"

"My head. . .hurts."

"Detective, is it okay if we stop the questioning for a few minutes while I get Karen some Tylenol?"

"I don't mind at all."

Karen heard Pastor Smith's retreating footsteps as she closed her eyes and rubbed her aching head. Her pain worsened as she leaned back into the chair. Darkness, like a descending hoard of black birds, closed around her. *Lord, God, Almighty, I'm about to pass out.*

Order Bittersweet Dreams
https://ceceliadowdy.com/bittersweet-dreamslp

About Cecelia Dowdy

CECELIA DOWDY is an Amazon bestselling author who lives near Washington DC. She enjoys listening to old tunes with her husband and chauffeuring her teenaged son to his school sports events. Baking is one of her favorite passions. She loves experimenting with bread recipes using her sourdough starter. Serving homemade desserts to friends brings her joy. Her love of baking shines in her romance novels. When she's not in the kitchen, or spending time with her family, she's cooking up delicious faith-filled plots. Fans say reading her tasty novels makes them hungry. Sign up for her **newsletter**.

CONNECT WITH CECELIA DOWDY

I hope you enjoyed Milk Chocolate Kisses.

Join my mailing list!
I will keep you updated about future releases:
https://ceceliadowdy.com/sign-up-for-my-email-list/

Let's discuss the Bible – visit my Sunday Brunch
biblical discussions on my blog:
*http://ceceliadowdy.com/blog/category/sunday-
brunch*

Please visit my website for more of my books:
www.ceceliadowdy.com/

You can also find me on social media:

Facebook:
www.facebook.com/CeceliaDowdyAuthor

Twitter:
https://twitter.com/cdnovelist

Bookbub:
www.bookbub.com/authors/cecelia-dowdy

Other Titles by Cecelia Dowdy

THE BAKERY ROMANCE SERIES
http://ceceliadowdy.com/bakery-romance-series/

Loving Luke *(Book 0)*
Raspberry Kisses *(Book 1)*
Shades of Chocolate *(Book 2)*
Sweet Dreams *(Book 3)*
Sugar and Spice *(Book 4)*
Southern Comfort *(Book 5)*
Sweet Delights *(Book 6)*
Cinnamon Kisses *(Book 7)*

THE CANDY BEACH SERIES
https://ceceliadowdy.com/the-candy-beach-series2/

Caramel Kisses – *(Book 0)*
Chocolate Dreams – *(Book 1)*
Milk Chocolate Kisses – *(Book 2)*
Bittersweet Dreams – *(Book 3)*
Coffee and Kisses – *(Book 4)*
Rocky Road Dreams – *(Book 5)*

STANDALONE TITLES
http://ceceliadowdy.com/books/
The Bakery Bride

The Underground Railroad Brides Collection –
a historical romance novella collection
http://ceceliadowdy.com/underground-railroad-brides-collection/

Courting the Doctor
A Teachers Heart – a historical romance novella
collection
https://ceceliadowdy.com/a-teachers-heartlp/